Oxford
Progressive
English Readers

JUN 1 6 2006

Twenty Thousand Leagues Under the Sea

D1622663

The *Oxford Progressive English Readers* series provides a wide range of reading for learners of English.

Each book in the series has been written to follow the strict guidelines of a syllabus, wordlist and structure list. The texts are graded according to these guidelines; Grade 1 at a 1,400 word level, Grade 2 at a 2,100 word level, Grade 3 at a 3,100 word level, Grade 4 at a 3,700 word level and Grade 5 at a 5,000 word level.

The latest methods of text analysis, using specially designed software, ensure that readability is carefully controlled at every level. Any new words which are vital to the mood and style of the story are explained within the text, and reoccur throughout for maximum reinforcement. New language items are also clarified by attractive illustrations.

Each book has a short section containing carefully graded exercises and controlled activities, which test both global and specific understanding.

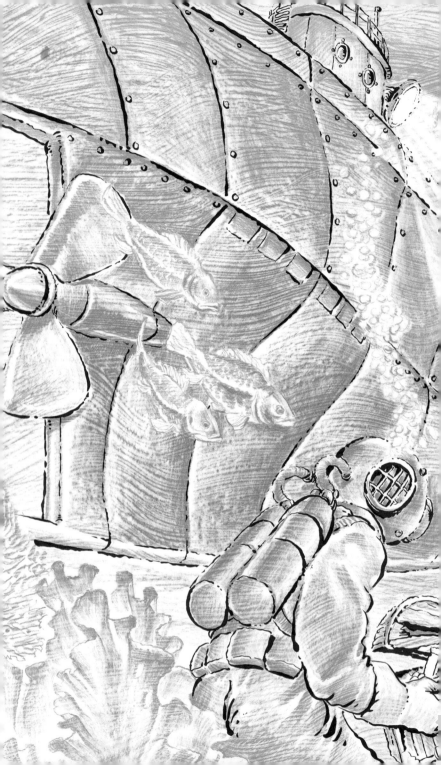

Twenty Thousand Leagues Under the Sea

Jules Verne

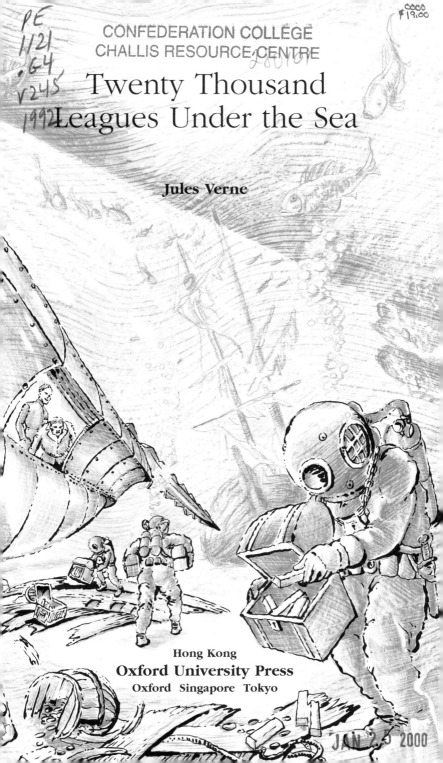

Hong Kong
Oxford University Press
Oxford Singapore Tokyo

Oxford University Press

Oxford   New York   Toronto
Kuala Lumpur   Singapore   Hong Kong   Tokyo
Delhi   Bombay   Calcutta   Madras   Karachi
Nairobi   Dar es Salaam   Cape Town
Melbourne   Auckland   Madrid

and associated companies in
Berlin   Ibadan

Oxford is a trade mark of Oxford University Press

First published 1992
Second impression 1994

Illustrated by K.Y. Chan

Syllabus designer: David Foulds

Text processing and analysis by Luxfield Consultants Ltd.

ISBN 0 19 585469 1

Printed in Hong Kong
Published by Oxford University Press (Hong Kong) Ltd
18/F Warwick House, Taikoo Place, 979 King's Road,
Quarry Bay, Hong Kong

CONTENTS

1

THE NARWHAL

A sea monster

My name is Pierre Arronax. I am the Assistant Professor at the Museum of Natural History in Paris. I am also the author of a well-known book called *Mysteries of the Ocean Depths*. The story that I am about to write describes some of these mysteries, and tells how I was able to see them with my own eyes.

In June 1866, I was sent by the French Government to take part in a scientific expedition to Nebraska, an unexplored region of the United States of America. I spent nine months there, and collected a large number of rocks, plants and animals for the museum.

In March 1867, I arrived in New York with my notes and my collection of specimens. I wanted to return to France as soon as possible, but before I could leave, I had to pack up my collection, and go to a few meetings. I was also asked to give one or two lectures.

I decided, therefore, to take rooms in a hotel for myself and Conseil. Conseil is my servant, and also my scientific assistant. I found a good hotel and we started work. I gave three lectures which were praised by all who heard them. Conseil kept the plants and animals in good condition. I hoped that we would be able to leave at the beginning of April, but on 20th March, something happened which changed all my plans.

Everyone will remember that in July and August of 1866 several ships met a strange object in the sea. One ship, the *Governor Higginson*, came across it five miles off the coast of Australia. At first the captain thought he had found an unknown island, but suddenly two columns of steam shot thirty yards up into the air. He knew then that it was not an island, but he could not tell what it was.

Three days later, the crew on the *Columbus*, sailing across the Indian Ocean about 700 miles from Australia, saw the same thing. Fifteen days later, two more ships saw it in the North Atlantic. Both captains thought that it was larger than their own ships, about 100 yards in length.

Nobody could agree what it was. Some said it was a floating island, but they could not explain how it moved so fast. Others said that it was a sea monster, but nobody took that idea seriously. For a few months, the papers were full of amazing pictures and amusing jokes about monsters, and then the subject was forgotten.

Then, on 20th March 1867, when I was back in New York, the *Moravia* was crossing the Atlantic, with 237 passengers on board. She was sailing at a steady speed of fifteen knots (about seventeen miles per hour), when she struck something. The officers on the watch deck could see only a strong current 1,500 feet away. There were no rocks in that part of the sea, so they thought they might have hit an enormous wreck. They recorded its position carefully, and sailed on slowly.

They reached New York five days later. When the ship was examined, it was found that part of her keel had been broken off. If her hull had not been very strong, she would have sunk with all the passengers and crew.

When this happened, people were very worried, and began to wonder if the monster had come back. I was invited to give some lectures about creatures that live in the sea. When I was asked what had damaged the *Moravia*, I said that there was not enough evidence to decide. But secretly I thought that it might be a monster. I decided to stay in New York and see if anything else happened.

On 13th April, another ship called the *Scotia* was sailing at thirteen knots to Liverpool. At exactly 8.17 p.m., while the passengers were having dinner, a slight shock was felt. The chief engineer went down to see if the bottom of the ship had been damaged. He found that water was pouring into one of the divisions of the hold. Fortunately, it was possible to keep the water out of the other divisions, so the ship was not in danger. She was able to sail on slowly, and reached Liverpool a day late.

When the engineers in Liverpool examined her, they could hardly believe their eyes. Two and a half yards below the water line there was a large hole. It was triangular, and the edges of the hole were quite straight. Something had forced itself through an iron plate which was one and a half inches thick.

After this, it seemed that all ships were in danger. Even governments began to take the matter seriously. All the information about the strange object was collected together, and important people were asked to give their opinions.

There was very little information. The object was about 100 yards long and could travel at fifty knots for a long period of time. It could travel on the surface, and under the surface. It had a hard body, and carried some sharp weapon which could make a hole in iron.

Some people said that it was a submarine vessel, but this idea was not accepted. Firstly, every government said firmly that they had not made such a ship, and that they were certain no other government had made one.
5   Secondly, it was impossible for a private person to build such a ship. Even if he had a place to build it, or the money to pay for it, he could not have built it without someone knowing.

My theory

10   Most people said it was a monster. When I was asked for my opinion, I felt that I could no longer say that there was not enough evidence. But I did not want to be laughed at, so I wrote a careful letter to the *New York Herald*. This is part of what I wrote:

15   'Could a monster as large as this exist? Yes, it could, for there are many parts of the sea which we have never visited. We have no idea what lives at the bottom of the ocean.

'What would it look like? It might be very different from
20   anything that we have seen before. If it lived near the bottom of the ocean, it would have to be very large and strong, in order to resist the water pressure.

'But I believe that it is a huge specimen of a creature that fishermen meet quite often. I mean the narwhal. The
25   largest caught so far was twenty yards long. It had a bone sword at the front which was as hard as steel, and six feet long. If we can imagine a narwhal five times larger than that one, then we have a creature that fits the evidence so far.

30   'Therefore, unless new evidence is provided, I shall believe that the cause of these accidents is a giant narwhal, which is as strong and powerful as a warship. I must add, however, that it is possible that we are dealing with something quite different from what we have ever
35   imagined or experienced.'

My article was praised by everyone, and I was very pleased.

All now agreed that there was a monster, and the public called for action to find it and kill it, so that it could not put any more ships in danger.

The United States was the first country to take action, and in New York they made preparations for an expedition to catch the narwhal. A very fast warship, the *Abraham Lincoln*, was made ready. The commander, Captain Farragut, was allowed to put on board all the weapons and equipment that he wanted.

Within two weeks the ship was ready, but no one knew in what direction it should sail. For two months no ship saw the monster. People grew very impatient, until on 2nd July, they learned that a steamship sailing from California to Shanghai had seen it in the North Pacific Ocean.

Everybody was full of excitement. The *Abraham Lincoln* was once more made ready and loaded with food, water, and fuel for the engines.

Three hours before it left New York harbour, I received this letter:

Mr Pierre Arronax,
Assistant Professor at the Paris Museum of Natural
History
Fifth Avenue Hotel
New York

Sir,
If you will agree to join the Abraham Lincoln *in the expedition to find the narwhal, the United States government will be very pleased that a famous scientist from France is taking part. Captain Farragut has a cabin ready for you.*

Very sincerely yours,
J.B. Hobson
Secretary of the Navy

At first I could not decide what to do. On the one hand, I was tired after my recent travels. I wanted to see my house again, and continue with my scientific work. On the other hand, this was a great chance to find out what the monster was. Perhaps I would bring glory to France. Within a few minutes I made up my mind. I would go.

Next I had to ask Conseil if he would come with me. He had been with me on every expedition I had made in the last ten years. I expected, therefore, that he would agree, but I had to ask him, because this one might be both long and dangerous.

'Conseil!' I shouted.

'Yes, sir,' he said, entering the room.

'Ah, Conseil. I've been invited to join the expedition that will look for the narwhal.'

'Yes, sir.'

'Will you come with me?'

'Yes, sir.'

'Then pack our things. We leave in two hours. Put all my clothes and my scientific notebooks and instruments into one large box.'

'Yes, sir.' He left to begin at once.

While he packed, I made arrangements with the hotel to look after my specimens. Two hours after I had received the letter, we reached the ship. Some sailors carried the luggage on board, and I was taken to Captain Farragut.

'Are you Professor Arronax?' he asked me.

'Yes, I am. You must be Captain Farragut.'

'Yes. You are very welcome, Professor. Your cabin is ready for you.'

I went down to the cabin where Conseil was unpacking our luggage. It seemed very comfortable, so I left him to finish the work and went up on deck.

The ship was already leaving the harbour. A huge crowd of people cheered and waved their handkerchiefs. We moved down the river to the open sea, and were soon on our way.

The search for the monster

When land was out of sight, and we were sailing at full speed in the Atlantic Ocean, I went to talk to the captain.

'Good evening, Captain.'

'Good evening, Professor Arronax. How do you like your cabin?'

'It's very comfortable, thank you, Captain. This seems to be a fine ship. How fast can she sail?'

'Eighteen and one-third knots, Professor. She was chosen for her speed, and I am sure she will be fast enough to catch the monster. I have ordered the engineers to go at full speed, and we should be in the Pacific three weeks from now.'

I noticed that many of the sailors were already looking out to sea, and that some had climbed up the mast so that they could see better.

'The men seem very certain that we shall see the monster soon,' I said.

'Of course they are. Everyone is certain. And everyone hopes to win 2,000 dollars. I have promised to give that amount of money to the first person to catch sight of the monster.'

5   'You are determined to find the monster, I can see.'

'Absolutely determined, Professor. I shall find it, and either I will destroy the monster, or the monster will destroy me.'

'What weapon will you use, Captain?'

10   'This warship carries all the most modern weapons. We have a gun which fires harpoons, a larger one which fires bullets, and our largest gun of all can fire a heavy shell over a distance of ten miles.'

'Excellent!' I cried.

15   'But we also have on board the greatest harpooner in the world. I should like you to meet him.'

The captain called for Ned Land. When the harpooner arrived, the captain introduced us and then left us together.

A conversation with Ned Land

20   Ned was about forty years old, tall and strongly built. He was a French Canadian, and although he did not talk much to the other men, he liked to talk to me in French. Ned used to tell me stories of his adventures as a whale hunter, and we became good friends.

25   One day, when we had been at sea for three weeks, and were moving north in the Pacific Ocean, I asked Ned what he thought about the monster.

'Well, Ned,' I said, 'how long do you think it will be before we catch the monster?'

30   'A very long time, Professor, because I do not believe that such a monster exists.'

'Good heavens!' I cried. 'Why not? You must have seen many huge whales.'

'Yes, I have, but I've seen nothing that could scratch
35   the iron plates of even the smallest ship.'

'But Ned, there are stories of ships which the sword of a narwhal has cut through.'

'Those were wooden ships, not iron ones.'

'Well, Ned, I believe that somewhere there is a huge monster, like a whale, or a large dolphin, or a narwhal, which can move very fast, and has a sword that is strong enough and sharp enough to make a hole in iron.'

'Well, I don't.'

'But think of this. If such a monster exists, we have not seen it before because it usually lives at the bottom of the sea. And if it lives at the bottom of the sea, it must be very large and very strong, in order to bear the enormous pressure of the water. An ordinary creature could not live so far down.'

'Yes, I agree that if this monster exists, it must be very strong.'

'If it doesn't exist, Ned, what made that hole in the *Scotia*?'

Ned could not answer me.

Perhaps he did not believe that there was a monster, but Ned continued to spend all his time looking out to sea. So did I. I was not interested in the reward of 2,000 dollars, of course. But I did wish to make a scientific discovery which would bring glory to me and my country.

For three months we sailed the waters of the Pacific, and saw nothing but ordinary whales. We travelled along the coasts of America and Asia, and then sailed back across the middle of the ocean. We sent boats out at a distance from us, and followed a winding course, so that we might cover a larger area.

Gradually the crew became disappointed. Some said that we would never find a monster in the vast area of the Pacific Ocean. Others even began to say that there was no monster at all.

Captain Farragut was willing to search for the monster for years, but he had to think about the feelings of the crew. On 2nd November he announced that they would continue to search for three more days. If by the end of that time they had seen nothing, they would return home.

This decision pleased everybody. All the crew began to look out for the monster more eagerly, and we all stayed on deck hoping to be the first to see it.

On the second night Conseil came to watch with me.

'Ah, Conseil, so you have come up to see if you can win the 2,000 dollars.'

'No, sir, that is not my purpose. No one will win the 2,000 dollars.'

'I'm afraid you're right, Conseil. We shouldn't have come on this voyage. We should have gone back to France. We could have been there six months ago.'

'Yes, sir. You could have written your book about the expedition to Nebraska by now.'

'Oh dear. I'm afraid we shall be laughed at for going on this voyage.'

'Yes, sir. People will certainly laugh at you, sir, and if I may say so, sir...'

'Yes, Conseil, what do you want to say?'

'You deserve to be laughed at, sir. A professor should be intelligent, sir, and not say things or do things which...'

At that very moment Ned Land shouted out, 'Look over there! Look — the very thing we have been searching for!'

THE MONSTER IS FOUND

We see the monster

When Ned Land shouted that he could see the monster, everyone rushed to the deck. The captain ordered the engines to stop. Since it was night, I did not expect Ned to have seen anything, but when I looked in the right direction, there it was. Ned had won the 2,000 dollars. The monster was very large. Its wet skin was shining in the moonlight, but there also seemed to be a strange light coming from it. It was moving towards us, slowly.

The captain at once ordered the engines to start again. He tried to move away from the monster, but the monster was too fast. After circling around us, it went away for about two or three miles. Then it came back at very great speed. 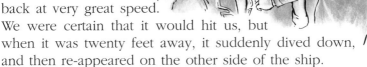 We were certain that it would hit us, but when it was twenty feet away, it suddenly dived down, and then re-appeared on the other side of the ship.

I went to speak to the captain.

'Why haven't you attacked?' I asked.

'It is too dark. I must wait until daylight, so that I can decide what parts to strike.'

'But what do you think it is?'

'I am quite certain that you're right and that it's a huge narwhal. I think also that it's an electric one. It seems very dangerous. We must keep a close watch on it all night.'

Only one thing happened during the night. At about midnight the light coming from the monster went out, and we wondered if it was still there. An hour later, however, there was a loud whistling sound, like steam escaping from a pipe. That told us the monster was still near.

We spent the night planning our attack. Ned Land asked the captain to prepare a small boat for him, so that he could get near and harpoon the beast. The officers brought the guns onto the deck.

By dawn we were all ready, but the thick mist prevented us from seeing anything. Once again, it was Ned Land who caught sight of the monster first.

When he pointed it out, we all saw a long black object in the water. Its tail beat the sea with great violence, turning the water behind it white. As it came nearer, I judged it to be about eighty yards long. Suddenly columns of water shot from two holes up into the air, making the noise we had heard in the night. Now we knew how it breathed.

The captain ordered the engines to go at full speed. We all cheered, because now we were going to attack. Black smoke poured into the sky, and the ship shook as the engines drove it through the water. In a few minutes we would be near enough to shoot.

We chase the monster

The monster, however, moved further off. For three-quarters of an hour it kept just ahead of us, although we went faster than ever before. We actually reached a speed of nineteen and a half knots, which was one knot over the safety mark. It was no use Ned Land going out in a boat, but he asked to be put out in front of the warship. From there, he could throw his harpoon when we got close enough.

But we never did. The monster not only kept ahead of us, but it went even faster, at about thirty knots.

We were all disappointed, especially Ned Land, who had won the 2,000 dollars for seeing the monster first, and now hoped to be the one to strike it. But the captain kept going.

'Fire the guns!' he shouted.   5

The first shot passed very wide, but the captain offered a reward for the first direct hit. Very soon we heard a loud explosion as a shell struck the beast.

'Full speed ahead!' ordered the captain, for he was certain that we should catch the monster now that it was   10 wounded. But to our astonishment, the beast showed no sign of tiredness or of injury. All day we pursued it. We covered 300 miles, but we were never close enough to fire again.

When night came, we lost sight of it, and we circled   15 slowly in the area where we were.

At 11.00 p.m. we saw the light appear again, and we sailed towards it slowly. Ned was in his place at the front of the ship, and we all watched to see what would happen. We sailed closer and closer.

                                                           20

I fall into the sea

Ned threw his harpoon. It struck the creature with a loud noise, but did not stick into the skin. All that happened was the light from the monster went out, and the giant creature sank below the waves.   25

For a minute, it seemed, everything was still and quiet. Where the monster had been there was just clear, empty water. Then, suddenly, without any warning, the front part of the warship rose high into the air, and then crashed down again deep into the waves. The monster had   30 attacked from below. Streams of water poured all over the ship. A huge wave swept across the deck and threw me into the sea.

Fortunately I am a good swimmer. I sank many feet below the surface, but soon came up again. When   35

I looked for the ship,
however, it was already
disappearing into the darkness,
trying to get away from the monster as fast as possible. I
5   was left alone, and certain to die, because my clothes were
pulling me under. Losing all hope, I cried, 'Help', and my
mouth filled with water. I sank down once more.

Just then a hand seized my clothes and pulled me up
to the surface.

10   'You were calling, sir. Please lean on my shoulder. You
will swim more easily.'

'Conseil!' I cried, holding his arm. 'Did the waves send
you overboard as well?'

'No, sir. I saw you fall into the sea, and so I dived in
15   after you.'

'Thank you, Conseil. Where's the ship?'

'I'm afraid it has gone, sir. Before I dived into the sea
I heard some sailors say that the rudder was broken.'

'Broken?'

20   'Yes, sir. Broken by the monster's teeth. The ship is not
damaged in any other way, but she cannot turn, and so
she cannot come back to this spot.'

'Then we'll drown.'

'Perhaps, but not yet. We can swim for a few hours, if we take off our clothes. Please let me cut your clothes away from you.'

With his knife, he freed me from my clothes, and I helped him get out of his. It was much easier to swim now. We took it in turns for one to lie on the surface, while the other held him up. We changed positions every ten minutes, and in this way we kept afloat for two hours.

At 1.00 a.m. I felt very tired, and my arms and legs became stiff. I could no longer swim, and Conseil could no longer keep me afloat.

'Leave me now. Leave me now,' I said to him.

'Never, sir.'

The moon came out, and we could see the ship five miles away. I did not shout, for I knew there was no hope. But Conseil did, and I thought I heard a cry answer him.

'Did you hear that?' I whispered.

'Yes, yes.' He called again, 'Help, help!'

This time we did hear a human voice. Conseil began to swim with new energy. He called again, and I seemed to recognize the voice that replied, but then I sank down for the third time.

As I went down, something hard hit me. I held on to it. Somehow it brought me to the surface of the water, and then I fainted. When I opened my eyes, I saw Conseil and, to my astonishment, Ned Land.

'Ned!' I whispered. 'What are you doing here?'

'Looking for the monster, Professor. And I have found it. When I fell off the ship, I was lucky, because I landed on this floating island.'

'Floating island?'

'Perhaps you would call it a giant narwhal. But I now know why my harpoon did not enter its skin.'

'Why, Ned. Why?'

'Because, Professor, its skin is made of iron.'

I was amazed. I rolled over and climbed further up out of the water onto this thing we were on. I kicked it.

It was very hard, so it could not be a narwhal or anything like that. Perhaps it had a shell. I touched it, but this shell was smooth. Part of the mystery was solved. The monster was a machine — a giant submarine.

Prisoners

So the monster was not a creature after all, but a ship made by people. One mystery was solved, but another mystery had begun. Who had built this vessel? Why did they build it? Why did they attack other ships?

There was no time to think about such things, for the ship began to move. We hung onto the upper part, and hoped it would travel on the surface. If it didn't, we should drown. All night we sailed in this way.

At last it became light. I began to look for some opening into the ship, but then it began to sink. Ned kicked it hard and cursed the men inside. It stopped sinking. A hatch slid open and a man came out. He took one look at us, and with a shout went back in. A few moments later eight men came out of the opening. They took us by the arms and pulled us down into the darkness.

They said nothing. As soon as we were inside the vessel, the opening was shut. We were made to climb down a steel ladder and walk a little way along a passage. Then we were pushed through a doorway. We heard the door shut, and we were alone in the dark. We were prisoners.

Ned was very angry indeed.

'These men are like savages,' he shouted. 'I expect they will eat us, but I shall fight them first.'

Conseil as usual was calm.

'They have saved us from drowning,' he said, 'and this room is quite warm. They have not harmed us yet. We must wait and see what happens.'

I began to move about the room to find out what I could about our prison.

'Fighting is no good,' I said to Ned. 'There are too many of them. We would be wiser to explore our new home. Come and help me.'

We carefully examined the room. We could find no doorway or window. The floor was covered with a carpet, and the ceiling was too high even for Ned to reach. The only furniture seemed to be a table and several chairs. We sat down and listened, but we could hear nothing at all.

For half an hour we sat in the darkness. Then quite suddenly a light came on. Ned took out his knife.

'Now I can see who is coming to attack me,' he said, looking very fierce.

'We must wait,' said Conseil. And we did so, wondering all the time what the ship was, who the men were, and what was going to happen to us.

After fifteen minutes, to our delight, a door opened and two men came in. The first was not very tall, but he was very strong, with broad shoulders. Ned stepped forward to meet him, pointing his knife at him. Then Ned stepped back, for he saw the second man.

The strange language

This man was very tall, and looked at us in a way that
made us afraid of him. His eyes were so far apart that he
seemed to see everything at once. When he looked
5   straight at us, we felt that he could see right through us.
He looked at each of us very carefully, but said nothing.
After a few moments he spoke to his companion in a
language I did not know. Then he looked at me and
10   seemed to ask a question.

I said in French that I did not know his language. He
still said nothing, so I went on talking. I explained who
we were, and described all our adventures. When I had
finished, he still said nothing.

15   I turned to Ned, and asked him to tell our story in
English. Ned spoke very clearly, but still the men did not
say anything, or show that they understood.

Conseil then offered to try German. Still they seemed
not to understand anything he said, so I tried Latin. The
20   two men simply looked at each other and went out of
the door.

Ned was very angry.

'We have spoken in four languages, and they don't even
speak to us,' he complained.

25   'Be calm,' said Conseil.

'I cannot be calm. I am very hungry, and I am sure that
we shall starve.'

'We may starve, but not for some time yet,' said Conseil.

I made a suggestion.

30   'Wait until the men harm you, before you judge them
to be bad.'

Ned was going to reply when the door opened again,
and a man brought in some clothes. We put them on, and
watched him lay the tables with knives and forks, and set
35   dishes of food and jugs of water on it. We sat down to
eat and found all the food very good, though we had
never tasted some of the things before. I was particularly

interested in the knives and forks, each of which was marked with the letter 'N'.

When we had finished our meal, we felt better and much more cheerful. It seemed that the men on this ship would take care of us after all. We felt tired, and laid ourselves down on the thick carpet. We were soon asleep.

We must have slept for a long time, because when we woke up we were completely rested, after all the troubles of the day before. We were sure that we would soon have another meal, and that we would see someone who could talk to us.

But we were wrong. First we began to find it very difficult to breathe. There seemed to be no air in our prison. Perhaps the ship had been under water for a long time, and now needed to return to the surface. Perhaps it was only our room that was short of air. Very much afraid, we lay on the floor and expected to die.

Suddenly the vessel began to rock, which showed that we were now on the surface. Very soon, fresh air was blown into the room, and we recovered.

The next trouble was that we had no food. We were very hungry, because we had slept for perhaps twenty-four hours, and no one had brought us anything to eat. Ned became so impatient, I was afraid that when someone did appear, he would fight them.

Ned started to shout, but there was no reply. Nobody came, and Ned got more angry. I was very worried. Only Conseil was calm.

THE *NAUTILUS*

Captain Nemo

After some hours, the door opened and a sailor looked in. Ned leapt at him, threw him to the ground, and seized his throat. Conseil rushed to help the man, and I tried to
5 pull Ned away. We were stopped by a voice which said in French, 'Leave that man alone, Mr Land, and you, Professor, stand up. Will you all please listen to me.'

10 It was the tall man with the strange eyes. He looked at us for some time, and we just stood there, waiting. I was so surprised that he should speak French. Eventually he spoke again.

'Gentlemen,' he said, 'I can speak French, English,
15 German, Latin, and other languages also. I could have answered you at our first meeting, but I wished to find out about you, and then to think carefully what to do. You all told the same story, and so I know who you are, and why the *Abraham Lincoln* pursued me.'

20 He paused, but we were so surprised we could think of nothing to say. Then he went on.

'I left you alone so long, because I wanted time to decide what to do with you. I do not want to meet anybody from the world again. I have cut myself off from
25 mankind. I feel that the easiest thing would be to leave you to drown. I do not like people to disturb me.'

'But we did not mean to disturb you!' I cried.

'Then why did your ship fire its guns at me? Why did you, Mr Land, strike my ship with your harpoon? You are
30 my enemies.'

'But we did not know that this was a ship. We thought it was a monster like a giant narwhal. We wanted to destroy it, because it was putting our ships in danger.'

'But if you had found out that this was a ship, your captain would still have tried to destroy it. It is my right to treat you as enemies. If I had left you to drown, I do not think I would have regretted it for a moment.'

'But that would be against the laws of civilized society,' I protested.

'I have cut myself off from civilized society. I want nothing to do with the human race and its laws. Society is unjust and the laws are useless.'

These words told me that we were dealing with a man who had no conscience. He was afraid of no man, and perhaps not even God. I could not think of any argument to put forward. After a long silence, the tall man continued to speak.

'I will, however, show you pity. You may stay on this vessel, since by chance you have come into it. But at times you must be locked in your cabins, so that you do not see certain things which may need to be done. If I order you to remain in your cabins, you must obey me. If you resist, then you will be killed.'

'I should like to ask one question,' I said.

'Please do so.'

'You say that we will be free to go about on board, except at these special times.'

'You will be quite free.'

'But when may we leave the ship?'

'Never. I am willing to keep you alive, but I will not let you return to the world, and give information about me and my ship. Do you accept my terms?'

'Yes, we accept them as long as we are on the ship, but we will never stop hoping that we may leave it one day.'

'Very well. I don't think you will regret spending the rest of your life on board. You, Professor, have written a book about the oceans and what is in them. I will be able to show you what life beneath the surface of the sea is really like.'

I was so pleased to think that I would be able to visit places under the sea, that I did not worry about losing my freedom. I felt that I could deal with that in the future. For the moment, I could think of only one further question to ask.

'What is your name? What should we call you?'

'You should call me Captain Nemo. I am the captain of the *Nautilus*.'

Captain Nemo then called for a sailor.

'Please show Mr Land and Mr Conseil to their cabin. Breakfast is waiting for you there, gentlemen. Professor, please come with me. We shall have breakfast together, and afterwards I will show you round my ship.'

More like a palace than a ship

Captain Nemo led me along a passage into an open space. We passed a steel ladder that led up to the roof, and I guessed that this was where we first entered the ship. I followed the captain through a doorway, and found myself in the captain's dining-room.

The room was brightly lit and beautifully furnished. There was a polished table in the middle of the room, and our breakfast was laid on it.

We sat down to eat, and after a while Captain Nemo spoke.

'How do you like this food, Professor?' he asked.

'I find it delicious, but it tastes quite different from ordinary food,' I replied.

'I'm glad that you like it. It all comes from the sea. We have stopped eating food from the land and are never ill now. That is one good reason for living in the sea. But the most important reason is that in the sea there are no unjust governments to make life miserable for people.'

He seemed to be thinking deeply, so I said nothing in reply.

After breakfast, he showed me into the library, which was next door. After a few moments, Captain Nemo looked at me.

'Well, Professor? How does this library compare with the library in your museum?' he asked. 5

'The museum library is not nearly so comfortable, and it does not have so many books,' I answered.

'Yes, there are over 12,000 books here. I hope you will enjoy reading them.'

Both the library and the dining-room were very 10 pleasant, but the sitting-room was the most beautiful. It was next to the library, and twice as large. Two of the walls were covered with famous paintings. All around were glass cases filled with things that the captain had collected. Beside one wall there was an organ. I began to 15 feel that the *Nautilus* was more like a royal palace than a ship.

When I looked closely at the glass cases, I saw plants and rocks of every size and colour, and most beautiful of all, a large number of pearls. Some of these were very big, and must have been worth at least half a million dollars each. While I was looking at them, Captain Nemo sat down at the organ and began to play. 25

At length he got up and said, 'I am very proud of this collection, Professor, for I gathered every single thing that you see with my own hands. I hope to add to it on the journey that we are going to make.'

The collection made me so excited that I found the 30 courage to ask the captain a question.

'The furniture, the pictures and the specimens show that you have a good knowledge of science and the arts, Captain. But you must also be a very skilful engineer. Would you please tell me what these instruments are for?'

I pointed to a row of clocks and bells on one of the walls.

'Of course, Professor, but I can explain their use more easily if we go into my room.'

We went out of the sitting-room into a short passage. The captain opened the second of two doors and said, 'This will be your room, Professor. It is next to mine.'

I looked inside quickly, and was pleased to see that it was very comfortable, and contained all the furniture that I could want.

The ship's instruments

The captain's room was quite different, however. The white walls were bare except for a row of instruments, which were the same as the ones I had seen in the sitting-room. The only furniture was an iron bed, a chair, and a large table, on which papers and maps were spread out.

'These clocks and bells are the instruments which enable me to guide the *Nautilus*,' Captain Nemo explained. 'They tell me the speed, the depth, and the direction of the ship, and any other information that I need. When I want to alter the speed, or give any command to my crew, I need only press a button or turn a handle.'

'But how does it all work?' I asked in astonishment.

'Everything on this ship is driven by electricity. Electricity provides the power to push the ship through the water, to pump air or water into the tanks, to light the ship and to cook the food.'

'But how do you obtain so much electricity?' I asked.

'I think that you had better come with me, and see the engine-room,' replied the captain.

We stepped once more into the short passage, and made our way back through the rooms that I had already seen. When we were in the central space, I noticed a smaller ladder going up to the roof, and a door that led into a steel cabin. I asked the captain what was there. 5

'The ladder goes up to the ship's boat. When the ship is under water, we use the boat to get to the surface. We use the steel cabin when we want to leave the ship and walk on the sea floor. You will soon be using them both yourself.' 10

There was no end to the wonderful things invented by this remarkable man. We went down a passage, and passed Ned and Conseil, who were still eating their breakfast in their cabin. We looked into the kitchen and the bathrooms, but not into the crew's cabin, so I could 15 not tell how many men were on board.

When I had seen over the engine-room, Captain Nemo took me back to the library, where we smoked cigars. I asked him more questions about the ship. He answered them willingly, because, he said, I would never leave the 20 ship.

After an hour or so, he looked at his watch.

'It is time to take our position, Professor. We must know exactly where we are before we start this journey. Please come up onto the platform with me.' 25

The roof of the central space was open. We climbed up the staircase and I found myself once more in the open air. While Captain Nemo took our position by the sun, I looked around me.

The platform we were standing on was only three feet 30 out of the water. It was surrounded by an iron railing. The ship's boat was positioned in the middle of the platform. Ahead of the platform, towards the front of the *Nautilus*, I learned later that there were two round glass windows. One was the window of the steersman's cabin, and the 35 other protected the light that shone ahead of us in the dark, or when we were under water.

'Twelve o'clock,' said Captain Nemo.

'Our position is fixed. In the distance over there you can see the coast of Japan. We will now sail at twenty-five knots — or about twenty-eight miles per hour — 150 feet below the surface. You can follow our course on the maps in the sitting-room. Now it is time to go down below.'

I went down the staircase and made my way into the sitting-room. There I examined the maps and tried to work out where we would go. Very soon, we were under the surface and our journey under the sea began.

How did the captain build the ship?

After half an hour, Ned and Conseil found me. They were amazed by the beauty and comfort of the room. Conseil went at once to the glass cases, and studied the collection of specimens. Ned came and sat down opposite me.

'Now, Professor. Who is this man? I've never heard of anyone called Nemo.'

'No,' I replied. 'You haven't. It's not his real name. It's a Latin word. It means "nobody".'

'Did you find out anything about him?'

'No, I'm afraid not, but he told me how he built the *Nautilus*.'

'How?'

'By ordering different parts from different countries, and putting them all together on a desert island.'

'Did he say how much it cost?'

'The ship itself cost sixty million dollars, the furnishings and everything needed to make it comfortable cost eighty million dollars, and his art treasures cost 200 million dollars.'

'How could he get so much money?'

'He didn't say.'

'Perhaps he found some pearls and sold them, sir,' suggested Conseil, who came and sat beside us. 'Some of the ones in his collection must be worth a fortune. But I would like to know more about the ship. Did Captain Nemo show you how it works, Professor?'

'Yes, he did. I can't explain it to you, but all the power is produced by electricity. He has invented a way of producing enough electricity to drive the ship at fifty knots for several months, without stopping. Electric power heats and lights the ship, and drives the pumps.'

'What are the pumps for, sir?'

'Some are used to work the supply of fresh air. Others empty and fill the tanks with sea water, and this allows the ship to rise and sink.'

'You mean that when he wants the ship to go down, he pumps water into the tanks. And when he wants the ship to go up again, he makes it lighter by pumping the water out.'

'That's right, Conseil. It seems so simple, doesn't it?'

'But do you think we are safe?' asked Ned.

'Completely safe, as far as I can tell,' I answered. 'The captain says that the ship is so strongly built that it will not be damaged by any accident. It is safe even in the most violent storm, because it can sail far below the surface, where the water remains calm. In addition, he gets all his food from the sea, so he never needs to go on land at all.'

'So how are we going to escape?' asked Ned.

'I think that we shall have to wait and see what happens,' I replied.

'What! Wait until he crashes into another ship and makes a hole in its side?'

'Captain Nemo assured me that he hit the *Moravia* and the *Scotia* by accident.'

'I don't believe him.'

'Anyway, Ned, we are now sailing into the ocean away from land, so we have no choice but to wait. In the meantime, we can read and study.'

'Perhaps you can, but I can't. I want to get out of this prison. I am tired of not being able to see anything.'

Just as Ned spoke, the wall on one side of the room seemed to open up. We all leapt to our feet, thinking
10 that the sea was about to pour in. But the sea was held back by a glass window that must have been amazingly strong. A light shone out from the *Nautilus* into the water, and there, right in front of us, we saw so many different kinds of creatures that Ned forgot about escaping.

15 We spent three hours looking out into a world that I had never dreamed of seeing. All sorts of fish swam past the window, their colours lit up by the very powerful lamp. Ned just sat and looked. Conseil busily made a note of all the different fish he saw. I was content to watch
20 their movements, and think how fortunate we were to be there.

Suddenly the two doors on either side of the window slid shut and blocked our view. We thought that Captain Nemo would join us, but he did not come. Soon Ned and
25 Conseil returned to their cabin, and I went to my room. There I found a delicious meal waiting for me. I spent the evening reading, writing and thinking. Then I felt very sleepy, and stretched myself on my bed. I slept well, while the *Nautilus* sailed steadily through the ocean depths.

4

ON THE FLOOR OF THE OCEAN

Invitation to a hunt

The next day was 9th November. We spent it by ourselves, and filled our time studying the collection of specimens in the cases, and watching through the window when the doors slid open. Meals were provided at the usual times, 5 and we were as comfortable as we could wish. After that, most days followed the same pattern, and this went on for several weeks.

During this time, the *Nautilus* sailed through the Pacific Ocean. We were able to follow the course that 10 Captain Nemo took, because our position was plotted each day on the maps in the sitting-room, and the instruments showed its direction and speed. In this way, we always knew where we were, but we never knew where we were going. 15

We sailed east-north-east for some days, as far as the island of Crespo. From there we made our way more or less south, down the middle of the Pacific, passing various islands such as Hawaii and the Marquesas. When we reached the Tropic of Capricorn, we turned west, passing 20 the Society Islands, Tahiti, and the New Hebrides group, until we reached the coast of Australia. Thus we travelled a huge distance in a remarkably short time.

We met no ships and never stepped on land. The *Nautilus* was therefore our prison. As I had expected, we 25 were free to do what we liked on the ship, but we had no chance of leaving it.

We learned nothing more about the crew, except that they spoke a language to each other that none of us knew. We saw the sailors so rarely that we were unable to learn 30 any words.

We learnt just as little about Captain Nemo. In fact, we hardly ever saw him. During the whole time we sailed in the Pacific, we spoke with him on only three occasions. The first was when we were near the island of Crespo.

5   After we had been in the *Nautilus* eight days, I found a letter in my cabin. Inside it was the following invitation:

To Professor Arronax, on board the Nautilus, *16th November 1867.*

Captain Nemo invites Professor Arronax to a hunting
10   *party, which will take place tomorrow morning in the forests of the island of Crespo. He hopes that the Professor will be able to join him, and he will be very glad if the Professor's companions can come with him.*

15   When I read this to my friends, Ned was delighted.

'A hunt!' he exclaimed. 'And on dry land too. Perhaps we shall have a chance to escape.'

'Let us first see where the island of Crespo is,' I suggested, leading the way to the maps. 'Ah, here it is.
20   Miles from anywhere and very small. Even if we do step on dry land and escape from Captain Nemo, I don't see how we can keep away from him, or get back to the mainland.'

'Perhaps not,' Ned said, 'but we may see some wild
25   deer or wild pig. They would make a very nice change from fish and seafood.'

In the morning, I went to the dining-room as usual, and found Captain Nemo there already.

'Good morning, Professor. Come and have breakfast
30   with me. Eat as much as you can, because it will be a long time before you eat another meal.'

I sat down and began to eat. After a pause, the captain spoke again.

'Professor, today we are going to hunt under the sea.'
35   'Under the sea!' I exclaimed. 'How?'

'We shall wear special diving suits, and we shall each carry our own supply of air on our backs.'

I could say nothing because I was so surprised. The captain went on.

'Not long ago two Frenchmen invented a way of forcing a large quantity of oxygen into iron bottles, and I have improved on their design. These bottles of oxygen allow us to breathe under water. We shall be able to walk freely for twelve hours without having to return to the ship.'

'But how can we see anything, and how can we throw a harpoon? It will be dark below the water, and we cannot throw anything if we are carrying heavy iron bottles.'

'Wait and see, Professor. I have developed a lamp which burns a chemical called sodium, and a gun that fires electric bullets. These bullets will kill any creature that they hit, however big it is.'

After breakfast we went to the centre of the ship. Here we found Ned and Conseil and several sailors. They were looking at some diving suits.

'I don't want to put on one of these,' said Ned firmly.

'But Ned,' I said, 'the forests of Crespo are under the sea.'

'Then I will just stay here.' He walked away looking very disappointed.

'What about you, Conseil? Are you going to put one on?' I asked my servant.

'My job is to follow you, sir.' And with these words he began to climb into a suit.

The suits were uncomfortable, and very heavy. The helmets were put over our heads, and screwed down into a metal collar. There were three windows in the helmet, so we could see in front and to each side. As soon as the helmet was in place, a bottle was fastened to our backs, and air flowed in. A gun and a lamp were put into our hands. We were ready.

As the suits were so heavy, we had to be carried into the steel cabin. The doors shut behind us, and the room began to fill with water. As soon as the room was full, another door opened, and we walked freely onto the sea bed.

It was an amazing feeling to be on the sea bed, thirty feet below the surface. At that depth, the sunlight still reached us, so we could see everything clearly for a distance of about 450 feet. Beyond that everything was dark blue.

First I took a good look at the *Nautilus*, which was now resting peacefully on the sand. The whole ship was smooth and black, and looked very like a giant narwhal. At one end was the long steel point which had done so much damage to the *Scotia*. At the other end was a rudder built in the shape of a fish's tail.

It seemed strange that we should be able to live inside that silent monster, and to have done so in safety for several weeks. But the journey that we now took was even stranger.

The forests of Crespo

Walking was easy. The sea bed was covered with all sorts of shells, rocks, plants and flowers. There were so many different colours — green, yellow, orange and violet — that I longed to be able to paint some pictures. Above us, seaweed moved gently, and all around tiny fish swam in and out of the rocks. In places we could see crabs and various shellfish. The only thing we could not do was talk to each other. Instead, I sang at the top of my voice, because I was so happy.

The floor of the ocean sloped gently down. After some time, we came to an area filled with enormous tree-like plants. I decided this must be the forest of Crespo, and it now became necessary to use our lamps. It was just like moving through a forest at night. The only difference was that the branches of the trees went straight up towards the surface, instead of spreading out.

Although we walked for four hours, I did not feel at all hungry. I did, however, feel very sleepy, and was very glad when Captain Nemo signalled to us to sit down. As soon as we did so, we fell into a deep sleep.

I don't know how long we slept, but it must have been for a few hours. I was beginning to stretch my legs and arms, when I saw something that made me get to my feet very quickly.

A few steps away, a huge sea spider, about three feet high, was looking at me and getting ready to jump. It could not hurt me, since my suit was too thick for it to bite through, but I was very glad that Captain Nemo had already seen it. He shot it dead with his gun. The terrible creature sank at once to the floor and lay on its back with its thick hairy legs waving in the water. We were quite safe, but I remembered that we might meet other more dangerous creatures.

25

I took more care to look around me, and hoped that Captain Nemo would go back to the ship now, but he went on. I was certain that huge monsters would see our light, but if they did, they kept away. Eventually we came to a wall of rock and we stopped here. This was the foundation of the island of Crespo, and Captain Nemo would go no further.

We returned by a different route, steeper and more difficult to climb. We saw many kinds of small fish, and had our guns ready to fire at anything dangerous or useful. Captain Nemo was the only man who fired a shot. He killed a beautiful animal whose golden fur must have been worth a great deal of money. He also managed to hit a huge bird which he saw flying just above the waves.

I became more and more tired, and was thankful to see the ship again in front of us. The air in my iron bottle seemed to be getting used up, and I looked forward to getting on board again. Suddenly, Captain Nemo took hold of us. He forced us down to the ground and lay down beside us. I looked up and saw two huge shapes pass by. I was horrified to recognize two sharks of the most dangerous sort, with enormous teeth and powerful tails. Fortunately they do not see well, and they passed without touching us. When it was safe, we walked the last few yards to the ship, and were soon inside again.

That was the only time we left the ship while we sailed through the Pacific. Later we saw most of the creatures again, through the window in the sitting-room. But after that I could never look at sharks or sea spiders, without remembering how afraid I had been in the forests of Crespo.

Wrecks

Looking through the window was our main pleasure, but one day we saw a dreadful sight. Conseil saw it first. I was reading, and he called me over to look at a huge black shape on the sea bed. As we came close,

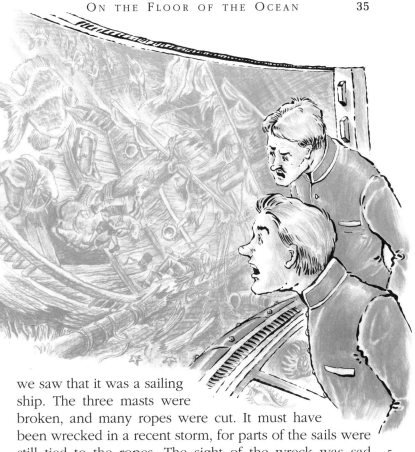

we saw that it was a sailing
ship. The three masts were
broken, and many ropes were cut. It must have
been wrecked in a recent storm, for parts of the sails were
still tied to the ropes. The sight of the wreck was sad   5
enough, but worse still we saw some dead bodies tied to
the ship. One was a woman. She was holding a little child,
and her hair flowed out all around her. The steersman was
was still tied to his wheel. As we left, we could see the
name of the ship, the *Florida*, from Sunderland.   10

We often sailed close to the ocean floor, and saw many
wrecks of ships that had sunk. Sometimes we were able
to guess what had happened. But Captain Nemo never
stopped to look. The only ships that he was interested in,
we discovered — on the second occasion we spoke to   15
him — were the ones that left France in 1785, on a voyage
round the world.

Everyone knows that the two ships, the *Boussole* and the *Astrolabe*, left France in 1785 under the command of Captain La Perouse, and were never seen again. Many people believed that the ships had been wrecked somewhere in the Pacific, and in 1827, they were found lying in deep water in the bay of Vanikoro. The natives on the island at first refused to say anything about what had happened, but after some time one of them told the story. Most of the sailors had swum ashore. Some had stayed on the island and eventually died there. But the captain and some others had built a small boat and left. No one knew where they had gone, or what had happened to them.

No one, that is, except Captain Nemo. When we were near Vanikoro, he came to visit us. The *Nautilus* approached the spot where the wrecks could still be seen, though the wood and iron were covered with coral.

'Everyone knows that these ships lie here,' said Captain Nemo, 'but I have found the small boat in which La Perouse and his men left Vanikoro. It lies near the Solomon Islands. Have a look at this box.'

He opened an old tin box, and inside it lay some papers, on which were written the instructions of the King of France to La Perouse. There was also a diary.

'I found this box in the wrecked boat. La Perouse and his men lie under the sea in a bed of coral. I could not wish for a better resting place for myself.'

With these solemn words he left the room.

Cities under the sea

We did not see the captain again for some time. Our hunting expedition had shown us that Captain Nemo felt himself to be the owner of the oceans, and his comment about La Perouse showed that he hoped to be buried beneath the sea. The third occasion on which we spoke with him made clear his violent hatred of mankind.

We did not travel below the surface all the time. Not only did we have to renew the air in our reserve tanks, but we also collected our food on the surface. The men let out long nets, in which they caught fish and seaweed, and all kinds of living creatures. We usually went up onto the platform to watch the men bring in the nets. It was very pleasant to be in the fresh air, and we often saw the most amazing things.

On one occasion, the nets brought in half a ton of food of various types. The sailors were picking out the items they wanted, and this was a long task. Captain Nemo came up to us and said, 'There is enough food in the ocean to feed the whole population of the world. Sometimes I imagine entire cities being built below the sea. It would be wonderful to live in an undersea city. Life under the sea is calm, safe, and enjoyable.'

He paused, and seemed to be remembering some sad events, for he held his face in his hands and sighed loudly. Then he went on.

'But it would be no use. Some unjust ruler would seize power, and make life below the sea no better than life on land. We don't need new cities, Professor, we need new men.'

I very much wanted to ask him why he felt such a hatred of people. But I was afraid of making him angry, so I did not dare. I often asked the others what they thought, but they were not very interested in Captain Nemo's secrets. Conseil was content to study the specimens already in the collection, and the new ones discovered in the fishing nets. Ned said that he wanted only to step onto dry land, to eat roast meat, and above all, to escape. It was left to me to wonder in what country the captain had lived, and if the government had treated him badly in some way.

As things turned out, two of Ned's wishes were satisfied before I learned more about the captain's past life.

STUCK ON A ROCK

In the Torres Straits

By the time we reached the coast of Australia, we had travelled almost 12,000 miles, or nearly 4,000 leagues. This great distance had taken us just under two months. We then moved north along the coast and then north-west across the Coral Sea. From this, I guessed that Captain Nemo intended to pass through the Torres Straits and the Timor Sea, into the Indian Ocean.

The Torres Straits are 100 miles wide, but filled with many small islands and rocks. It is very difficult to pick a course through this channel, and the *Nautilus* went very slowly. Ned and I went up onto the platform to watch the progress of the boat, and all round we could see coral rocks, which would completely wreck any wooden ship that touched them. I had charts in front of me, and could see the spot where one ship had struck the rocks and sunk.

At first, I thought Captain Nemo was steering for the same spot, but then he changed course towards the Island of Gilboa. We approached quite near it, and could see the trees on its shores. Suddenly a shock threw me over. The *Nautilus* had struck a rock and she stayed fixed to it, lying slightly on one side. The ship was not damaged, being made of iron, but it could not move.

The tide was going out. When it came in again, the level of the water would rise, but not high enough for the ship to float off. It really looked as if the *Nautilus* would stay on that rock for ever.

Captain Nemo discussed the situation with his second-in-command. After some minutes he came up to me.

'Are we in danger?' I asked.

'Not at all,' he replied.

'But it looks as if your ship will never sail again. You will have to step onto the dry land that you hate so much, after all.'   5

'Professor, you are mistaken. In five days the moon will be full. On that day the tides will be higher than usual, and we will float off this rock. I am sure you will be glad that neither our voyage nor your life need end yet.'

With these words he left us.   10

I was glad that Captain Nemo was so confident that the *Nautilus* would float again, but I was sad when I realized that he had not changed his mind about us. He would not allow us to return to our own countries.

I told the others what the captain had said. Ned was   15
very determined.

'I do not believe that the ship will ever sail again,' he said. 'In fact, I am sure that we should try to escape now.'

'Where will you escape to?' said Conseil. 'That island is a long way from home. Perhaps there are strange,   20
dangerous animals on it. Perhaps the people there will kill us if they find us on their land.'

'Well I should still like to go there, and get something to eat.'

On the island   25

Ned persuaded me to ask the captain if he would permit us to take the boat to the island. To my surprise, he agreed, and gave us guns, axes, and other equipment for our expedition. He did not even make us promise not to try to escape. He probably knew that it was impossible.)   30

The next morning we set out. Ned steered the boat while Conseil and I took the oars. All of us were very pleased to leave our prison, even if it would only be for a short time. Ned was especially excited to think that he would soon eat real vegetables and real meat.   35

As soon as we touched the sand, Ned jumped out of the boat, ran to a tree, and struck down some large coconuts. We drank the milk from the coconuts, and ate the white flesh with great pleasure.

5   'This tastes much better than the food on the ship,' said Ned. 'I am sure that the captain will let us take some on board.'

'Yes, I think he will,' I replied, 'but I don't think he will eat any himself.'

10   'That will leave all the more for us,' said Ned.

'But we must see if there is anything else to eat,' said Conseil. 'What about some vegetables and some other fruit, and even some meat? I haven't seen any animals or birds yet.'

15   'You are right, Conseil. We should start to explore at once,' answered Ned.

For two hours we walked in the forest, and were lucky enough to see some small kangaroos, which we shot. Then we found several breadfruit trees. Ned Land knew these fruits well. He had eaten them often on his many voyages, and knew how to cook them. He was very eager to eat some, and so we stopped for a while.

Ned gathered some dead wood and lit a fire. Then he took the fruits which Conseil and I had picked out. After cutting them into thick slices, he put them in the fire. When the outside was roasted, he took the slices out of the fire and gave them to us to eat. The inside was delicious. We all enjoyed the meal.

Then, just as we finished, a stone fell at our feet.

'Where did that come from?' gasped Conseil. 'It did not come by itself, I am certain.'

Another stone hit his hand, so that he dropped a piece of breadfruit he was holding.

'Natives!' Ned cried.

We leapt to our feet, and put our guns to our shoulders. About twenty natives appeared. There were too many for us to fight.

'To the boat!' I shouted.

Our boat was twenty yards away. In a few moments Conseil and I reached it, and began to push it out into the water. Ned came behind us carrying the kangaroos, which he was determined not to leave behind. He threw them into the boat, and climbed in after us. Then we rowed away as fast as we could.

Fortunately the natives did not come close. They threw stones and sticks at us, but from too far away, and we were not hit. About 100 natives gathered on the beach. Some of them walked into the sea shouting at us and waving their arms, but we sailed further and further away from them, and were quite safe.

When we reached the *Nautilus*, I left the other two to tie up the boat and put away our store of food and equipment. I went at once to look for the captain. I found him in his sitting-room, playing the organ.

'Captain!'

He did not hear me.

'Captain!' I said again, touching his arm.

He gave a start of surprise, and turned round.

'Good evening, Professor. Have you had a good hunt?'

'Yes, Captain, but unfortunately some natives are hunting us.'

'Are you surprised? You find natives in every country. I expected you would meet some soon. How many have you seen?'

'At least one hundred.'

'Don't worry, Professor. They will never harm the *Nautilus*.'

He said no more and began to play again. I soon left, and reported to the others what Captain Nemo had said.
We went out onto the platform, and looked over to the island. It was not possible to see the natives, but we could see the fires that they had made. Clearly they did not intend to go away. Although Captain Nemo was confident that we would be safe, we felt very nervous.
We wondered what would happen if the *Nautilus* was attacked.

The natives come closer

We did not manage to sleep much that night, and at dawn we were back on the platform. There were many more natives now, about five or six hundred of them. Some had swum to the coral rocks quite near to the *Nautilus*. I could see that they were tall and strong, with black skins, and black hair. They wore ornaments of teeth and beads round their arms and necks, and carried bows, arrows, spears, and other weapons.

At high tide the natives left these nearby rocks, but we could not leave the *Nautilus*. Ned spent his time cooking kangaroo meat and storing our stocks of food. I decided to throw a net over the side of the *Nautilus*, and gather up as many specimens of shells and plants as I could. Conseil helped me, and we were very successful.

Once again, however, the natives caught us by surprise. I had just found something very valuable, a shell that twisted to the left instead of to the right. I had passed it to Conseil. He was looking at it, when a stone struck it and smashed it to pieces in his hand. He gave a cry of anger, seized his gun, and pointed it at a savage who was less than twenty yards away. I ordered him not to shoot. I said that a shell was not worth the life of a man. He obeyed me, but not at all willingly.

The natives had collected a number of canoes, which held about twenty men each. They had come quite close to the ship, but were still afraid of this iron monster. We crawled along the *Nautilus* on to the platform and went downstairs with all speed. I went again to Captain Nemo, and found him busy working on his calculations.

'Captain, please excuse my interrupting you, but the natives have obtained canoes. They will attack us very soon.'

'Then we must close the ship. I will give the necessary orders.'

He pushed a button.

'It will be done. You have nothing to worry about. The guns from your ship did not harm the *Nautilus*, so how can the spears of these natives harm her?'

'I agree,' I said, 'but we shall need to open the hatches to let in fresh air, and then it will be impossible to stop these natives from entering the ship.'

'Impossible, do you think? Well, we shall see. Please tell your friends that, whatever happens, we shall float off these rocks tomorrow afternoon at 2.40 p.m.'

I told Ned and Conseil what Captain Nemo had said, and then went to my own room, where I read and tried to sleep. But all night long I heard natives stamping on the platform, and making terrifying cries.

All that night and all the next morning we had to stay inside the ship. By 2.30 p.m. we were very anxious. The supply of air was running out, and we felt very sleepy and weak as we sat in the sitting-room, waiting to see if the ship would really move when the captain said it would. Suddenly the captain entered.

'You look ill, Professor. If you are short of air, then you will be glad to know that I have ordered the hatches to be opened. If you are worried, then I can only advise you to wait.'

'But you can't open the hatches. What about the natives?'

'They will never come in. Come and see for yourselves.'

We went to the staircase, and there we saw two members of the crew opening up the hatch. At once twenty fierce faces looked in. One native started to come
5   down the stairs, and I knew that we should have to fight. But the moment that the man touched the handrail of the staircase, he gave a cry of fear and jumped back, waving his hands. The others tried to take hold of the rail, and each one jumped back with a loud cry. Soon we could
10   hear them all diving into the water.

Ned was so pleased that he ran to the staircase, but as soon as he touched the rail, he also jumped back.

'I've been struck by lightning!' he shouted.

In this way, we learned why Captain Nemo had been so confident. The electricity which the ship used for light and power also protected it, for it passed through the handrail. When the electricity was switched on, the rail became live, and no one could touch it without getting a severe shock.

The natives had disappeared, and we, half laughing, comforted poor Ned, who still shouted and cursed.

30   Just at that moment, the *Nautilus* was lifted off the rock by the last wave of the tide. It was 2.40 p.m., exactly the time that Captain Nemo had said.

No questions!

Once we were free of the rock, we sailed steadily to the
35   west. Travelling at thirty-five knots, we passed the mouth

of the Gulf of Carpentaria and entered the Timor Sea. We
saw the island of Timor in the distance, and then followed
the coast of Australia for a little. It looked as if we might
sail south towards the Antarctic, but Captain Nemo
changed course and we sailed north-west into the   5
Indian Ocean.

In the open sea we did not travel so fast. Captain Nemo
tested the temperature of the water at different depths.
Ned spent much of his time cooking new sorts of food.
Conseil and I went on studying the creatures that we saw   10
through the windows, and examining the specimens that
we caught in the nets. We soon became used to our life
on board.

Each day I went up to the platform, when the ship was
on the surface. I used to watch the officer take the position   15
of the sun, and report to Captain Nemo.

On 19th January it was different. At midday
Captain Nemo appeared, carrying a telescope. The officer
was very excited, and pointed in a certain direction.
Captain Nemo looked through his glass. Then he turned   20
and walked up and down the platform. Every now and
again he would stop and look in the same direction.
Gradually his face became black with anger. Suddenly he
gave an order, and the *Nautilus* increased its speed
greatly.   25

I could see nothing, so I went down to the sitting-room
to get the telescope I kept there. I returned to the platform
and raised it to my eye. But at that moment it was knocked
from my hand.

I turned around, and was very afraid to see the captain   30
looking very angry. His eyes were wide open, and his
hands were raised above his head. I thought that he was
angry with me, but I realized that he was looking over
my head towards some point in the distance. He stood
quite still, and after a few minutes became calm again.   35

'Professor Arronax,' he said, 'I wish you to keep your
promise to me.'

'What must I do, Captain?' I replied.

'You and your companions must remain in a cabin until I allow you to come out.'

'We will, of course, but may I first ask one question?'

'No, sir, you may not.'

There was nothing more I could say, so I went down to tell Ned and Conseil what was going to happen. Ned was angry, but there was no time to argue. Four sailors came to the room and led us into the cabin. It was the same one in which we had been put when we first entered the *Nautilus*. The door was locked, and we were prisoners once again.

'Well, at least we have got something to eat this time,' said Ned, pointing to the table which was laid out for a meal, 'even if it is only fish and seaweed.'

We sat down at the table and ate in silence. Suddenly the light went out and we were in darkness. Ned fell asleep with his head on the table, and so did Conseil. I was a little surprised that they should fall asleep so quickly. Then I felt myself becoming sleepy, and realized that something had been put in our food.

I heard the hatches shut, and the noise of the ship going under water. I tried to stay awake so that I could hear what happened, but it was impossible. After a few moments, I knew nothing more.

When I woke up, I found myself in my own bed in my own room. I got up and tried the door. It opened, so I was no longer a prisoner. I went up to the platform, and found Ned and Conseil already there waiting for me. They had also woken up in their cabin. They had heard nothing, and seen nothing.

We could tell from the position of the sun that a whole day and night had passed while we were asleep. We could see no sign of anything that might have happened. The *Nautilus* was still in the ocean, and no land was in sight.

PEARLS AND A SHARK

Across the Indian Ocean

It was clear to Conseil and me that Captain Nemo hated men and the land on which they lived. But we did not agree about the reason for his hatred.

Conseil greatly admired him for his skill in building a ship like the Nautilus, for his scientific knowledge, and for his love of beautiful paintings, music and furniture. He thought that Captain Nemo had decided to keep away from men because some people had laughed at his brilliant ideas.

I thought differently. I felt that if Captain Nemo really hated all people, he would not have rescued us from drowning. I also wondered if perhaps there were some people whom he hated so much, that he wanted to destroy them.

Of course, the only person who could tell us who was right was Captain Nemo. But we did not dare to ask him, and we knew that if we did ask him, he would not tell us. We just had to wait and see if he did anything or said anything that would give us some information. The next hint came when we were by the island of Ceylon.

Our voyage through the Indian Ocean did not take us long. We sailed about 540 miles each day at a speed of twenty-two knots. Most of the time we sailed thirty feet below the surface, but each day we went up to the surface for air. Sometimes we sank deep down to a depth of two miles, or over 9,000 feet, but we never reached the bottom.

Ned Land did not enjoy the journey much, but he did a lot of cooking, which interested him. Conseil and I, on the other hand, found that every moment of every day

was filled with reading, or studying our specimens, or looking through the window in the sitting-room. I was particularly busy, because I had begun writing the story of my life. But for me, the best part of every day was
5   walking on the platform in the morning.

On 24th January we could see Keeling Island, and on 26th January we crossed the equator. Some of the wonderful things that we saw were huge, such as sharks, and albatrosses, which have longer wings than any other
10   sea bird. And then there were tiny creatures, called plankton, so small, that you could not see them without a microscope. But there were so many of them in the water, that the sea looked like milk.

The most horrible sight was a number of human bodies, that we passed floating in the Bay of Bengal. Captain Nemo was very sad when he saw them. He told us that the people had been drowned in floods on the River Ganges, and had been carried away into the sea.

Pearls

On 28th January, we reached the island of Ceylon. I was looking at the map when Captain Nemo came in to the
30   sitting-room.

'Professor, I expect you know that Ceylon is famous for its pearl fisheries.'

'Yes, I do, Captain. Are you going to sail to them?'

'No. I can't take the *Nautilus* so close to the land, but we can use the diving suits. I can take you and your friends there, if you would like to come.'

'I should like to very much, and I am sure the others would too.'

'There is just one thing, Professor. Are you afraid of sharks?'

'Sharks!' I exclaimed.

'Yes, Professor. Sharks. It's very likely that we shall meet some. Are you afraid of them?'

'Well, I don't know very much about them.'

'Oh, we are quite used to them. Anyway, we shall carry weapons, and we may be able to hunt some. That would be very interesting. I look forward to seeing you early tomorrow.'

When I was woken at 4.00 a.m., I dressed, and made my way to the sitting-room for breakfast. Here Captain Nemo joined me. He asked me if I was ready to start, and said that Ned and Conseil were already at the staircase.

We did not have to put on our diving suits for some time. The *Nautilus* could not go very close to the land, so we first of all climbed into the boat. Some of the crew had got it ready, and four of them rowed us to the pearl fisheries.

It was still dark, but after an hour's rowing, the sun came up and we could see the island of Manaar close to us. At 6.30 a.m., Captain Nemo ordered the men to stop rowing and drop the anchor. We then put on our diving suits and prepared to enter the water.

Captain Nemo explained that during the pearl diving season the bay was covered with little boats, and the sea was filled with divers looking for pearls. But the season had not yet begun, so we were the only people there.

I asked about the lamps that we had used on our journey off the island of Crespo, but the captain said that they were not necessary this time. I also asked about our guns, but Captain Nemo laughed and said we should carry only knives. He gave each of us one to put in our belt, but Ned carried his harpoon as well.

When we were ready, we climbed over the side of the boat and found ourselves standing in about four feet of water. Captain Nemo went ahead and signalled to us to follow. Gradually the water got deeper, and one by one we disappeared under the waves.

After walking for half an hour over rocks and sand, we reached the oyster bed. There were millions of them. Ned began at once to fill the bag he had brought with him, but Captain Nemo waved us on. He led us to an area of huge rocks, where large crabs watched us go by.

Among the rocks there was a large cave. Its roof and sides were formed of huge rocks, and the floor was covered in seaweed. As we went in, the light became less, but I could still see the great columns of rock which supported the roof.

I wondered why Captain Nemo had brought us here. Then he stopped, and pointed out a large object resting on a shelf by the wall. At first I thought it was a round rock, and then I realized that it was an enormous oyster. It must have weighed about 600 pounds, and it contained about thirty pounds of meat, enough to feed many people at a single meal.

The two shells were slightly open. The captain came near and put his knife between them, to prevent them from closing. Then with his hand he lifted up the flesh of the oyster.

There we could see a single pearl. It must have been the size of a coconut! It was perfect in shape and colour. I reached out my hand to lift it up and examine it closely, but Captain Nemo stopped me. He took away his knife and the shell shut again.

Then I understood his purpose. By some chance he had found this cave. It was too far for any diver to reach, so the oyster was quite safe. The water in the cave was still, so it could grow easily. Captain Nemo was leaving the pearl to grow bigger and bigger. I thought it would already be worth at least one million dollars.

This was what Captain Nemo had wanted to show us. Now we began to walk back to the boat.

After ten minutes, Captain Nemo stopped us suddenly. *5* He signalled to us to bend down near some rocks, and then he pointed to our right. I saw something moving. I thought at once of sharks, but it was not a sea creature. It was a man.

10

The shark attack

The man was an Indian fisherman who had come to dive early before the season began. I could see his canoe floating some feet above us. Again and again he dived, *15* gathered some oysters, and went back up. To help him he used a stone and a long, thin rope. One end of the rope was tied to the stone, the other end was tied to the canoe. When he went down, the fisherman held the stone between his feet. When he reached the bottom, he filled *20* up his bag with oysters, and then he let go of the stone, and floated up to the surface. He emptied the bag into the canoe, pulled up the stone, put it between his feet, and then went down again. Each dive lasted about thirty seconds. *25*

The diver never saw us. I pitied him because it seemed to be very hard work. He was never able to pick up more than ten oysters at a time, because they were stuck hard to the rocks. And many of the oysters would not contain any pearls. But I also admired him, because he worked *30* and dived so skilfully.

Suddenly I saw him leap up when he had only just come down. He was clearly terrified and I could see why. A huge shark was coming towards him with its jaws wide open. The Indian threw himself to one side and avoided *35* its teeth, but he was knocked down by the tail. The shark turned round to attack him again.

The Indian was certain to be torn to pieces. I was almost sick with horror. My legs went stiff and I could do nothing. But Captain Nemo rose
5 suddenly, walked straight towards the monster and prepared to fight it with his knife. The shark saw him. Leaving the Indian, it swam towards his new enemy.

Captain Nemo stood still and waited. Just as the shark
10 rushed to bite him, he threw himself on one side, and with great force pushed the knife into its body. But he did not kill the animal.

Blood poured out of the wound, and I could see nothing for a few moments. Then I saw the captain
15 hanging onto the creature, struggling bravely, and stabbing it again and again with his knife. Still he could not give it the final blow.

The shark then swam close to a rock, and forced Captain Nemo to let go. Badly shaken, he fell to the sea
20 bed. He pulled himself up in order to face the beast. But he was too late. The shark was on him. Its huge jaws were open ready to shut tight and cut the captain in half.

At that very moment, Ned struck it a death blow with his harpoon. There was more blood, and the shark moved
25 violently from side to side, but it was soon dead.

Captain Nemo went at once to the Indian who was still on the sea bed. He took him in his arms and, kicking the sea bed with his heel, rose to the surface. The three of us went up and held onto the fisherman's boat.

Captain Nemo put him inside it, and rubbed him until he showed signs of coming to life. Taking out of his pocket a bag of pearls, he placed it in the Indian's hands. Then we returned to the sea bed.

I often wondered what the Indian thought had happened to him. At one moment he was struck by a shark, and the next he was in his boat with a bag of pearls. What did he think were the four great copper and glass heads that looked at him over the edge of his canoe?

We could not speak to each other until we had reached our boat. Once on board, we took off our helmets with the help of the sailors. Captain Nemo spoke first.

'Mr Land, thank you for saving my life.'

'You saved mine once,' was all that Ned said.

The captain smiled but said nothing. We returned to the *Nautilus*, and passed the body of the dead shark on the way. It was more than twenty-five feet long, and was the type that has six rows of teeth. While we were looking at the object which had so nearly killed us, a dozen similar creatures appeared round it and began to tear it into pieces, and fight each other for the largest share. We were glad to leave them behind.

Later that afternoon I met the captain. I spoke to him about the adventure, and I shall always remember his reply. It was the next hint we had about his intentions and purposes.

'Captain Nemo,' I said, 'I should like to tell you how much I admired your courage this morning.'

'You are very kind to say so, Professor Arronax, but it was nothing. I could not watch that poor man being killed.'

'So you still have some love for people. You said that you want nothing to do with the world or with men, but you saved that man's life.'

'That man, sir, that Indian, is a victim of an unjust government. I was cruelly treated once, and now I try to help others who suffer the same treatment.'

A SECRET PASSAGE

The tunnel under the sea

After this, we sailed on to the Gulf of Oman, past the Laccadive Islands. We went near to the Straits of Oman, but did not enter the Persian Gulf. We kept moving west
5 on a line parallel with the Arabian coast.

Then we turned north, into the Red Sea, which was as interesting as I had hoped. There were many new specimens for Conseil and me to examine. But no opportunity to escape came our way, as Ned had hoped.
10 Ned often talked about escaping. One day he asked Conseil and me to promise to leave with him if the chance came. We agreed, but we really wanted to stay on the *Nautilus*. We could think only about all the wonderful things we might see under the ocean.

15 It was not long before we reached the cape which separates the Gulf of Aqaba from the Gulf of Suez. We sailed up towards Suez. I had a most interesting discussion with Captain Nemo, about the attempts made by man to build a canal to join the Mediterranean and the Red Sea.
20 We found that we both admired Ferdinand de Lesseps, the French designer of the Suez Canal. This canal was then being built. But Captain Nemo astonished me by saying that the *Nautilus* had no need of any canals to reach the Mediterranean.

25 'Do you mean that we will sail round Africa?' I asked.

'No. I mean that we shall sail through a tunnel that joins the two seas 150 feet below the surface.'

'A tunnel!' I exclaimed. 'Where is it?'

'In the rock below the sand.'

30 'But how did you know it was there?'

'Last year I noticed that several types of fish live in both the Red Sea and the Mediterranean. I marked a large number of fish in the Red Sea. Then I sailed round Africa and found some of the marked fish in the Mediterranean. This proved that there was a passage between the seas.   5

'After some weeks of exploration, I found it. The water flows at a great speed from the Red Sea to the Mediterranean. A few hours from now we shall be carried by that current through the tunnel.'

Although it was late at night, I stayed up to experience   10
this remarkable journey. At midnight, Captain Nemo took his place beside the steersman. I took up my position at the windows in the sitting room. I could see a huge black hole in front of us. It grew larger as we got nearer. The closer we got, the faster the water rushed past us. It carried us along with it, and the ship had to steady itself against the flow. Into the dark tunnel we went.

The lights of the ship showed up the smooth red rocks, unseen by any man except those carried by the *Nautilus*. I felt greatly honoured.

At 12.35 a.m. the tunnel began to grow wider. Captain Nemo turned towards me and said, 'The Mediterranean.'

We had passed under the Isthmus of Suez in twenty minutes.

5   ## Talk of escape

Next morning Ned came into the sitting-room to examine our position on the map. He was most surprised to see that we were in the Mediterranean.

'This can't be right,' he said. 'We were in the Red Sea
10 last night. The Suez Canal is not completed, and it would be too narrow for the *Nautilus* anyway.'

'Let's go up to the platform, Ned,' I said, 'and see what we can see.'

It did not take us long to climb the staircase and step
15 outside.

'There,' I said, pointing to the south. 'Do you recognize those buildings along the coast?'

'Yes, I do,' said Ned. 'That's Port Said. Have I been asleep for three weeks while we sailed round Africa?'

20 'No, just for one night. Captain Nemo used an unknown tunnel that joins the two seas 150 feet below the surface.'

'I am amazed, but I am very pleased, because we are getting nearer home. There was no opportunity for us to escape in the Red Sea, but the Mediterranean
25 should provide us with many chances. There are many islands, and I am sure that Captain Nemo will visit some.'

I did not feel very happy about this.

'Ned,' I said, 'I know we agreed to join you when we
30 had an opportunity to escape. But I don't want to leave the ship yet. Look at it this way. If we had escaped in the Red Sea, we should never have known about this tunnel. How many more wonders may we be shown in the Mediterranean Sea, in the Atlantic Ocean, and even in the
35 polar regions?'

'I don't know,' answered Ned, 'and I don't care either. We have sailed a long way, and today is the first time for three months that we have been in sight of civilization. There are many ports along the Mediterranean coast. It is quite likely that we shall pass near enough to one to make a successful escape. Once we are out in the Atlantic, we may have to wait many more months before we are near inhabited shores.'

'But we may sail north near France and England. And on the other side of the Atlantic there are the seaports in Canada and America. There may be lots of opportunities later.'

'There may be, but perhaps there won't be. We must take the chances that come now. We don't know where the captain plans to go. We don't know what he intends to do with us, except keep us prisoners. And this ship may even be destroyed in some accident.'

'Oh Ned!' exclaimed Conseil. 'That is impossible! The *Nautilus* is very strong, and the captain is so skilful a sailor that he will never make a mistake.'

'I agree that the ship is strong, and that the captain is a very skilful sailor. But I must point out two things. First, the captain is interested in exploration. He has already put the ship on a rock in the Torres Strait. He might take us somewhere else from which we could not get away. Second, there is always the unexpected. Something may happen which nobody can expect, because it has never happened before.'

'But unexpected things can happen on land too, Ned,' said Conseil.

'But you are safer on land than at sea. Seeing all the shipwrecks should remind you of that. We must try to escape as soon as there is an opportunity.'

'I suppose you are right, though I very much want to see the Atlantic. What do you say, Conseil?'

'I will do what you do, sir. I also would like to see more wonders of the sea, but I cannot say that Ned is wrong.

I think we should make plans for our escape, but I still hope it will be a long time before we have any chance.'

'So we agree to escape when we can, Ned. But we must be certain that our attempt will succeed. If Captain Nemo finds out, he will never give us the chance to escape again. He may even punish us in some way.'

'Yes, our first attempt must succeed. We will have the best chance when it is dark, and when we are near some European coast. If we are near the coast, we can swim. If we are too far away, or if the *Nautilus* is under water, we must use the ship's boat. I know how it works. All we do is climb inside, unfasten it, and shoot up to the surface. Nobody will notice us. I have already collected equipment and food. Both of you must make your own preparations, so that you can leave when the moment comes.'

'Well, we'll do as you ask, Ned. You may be sure of that. But I think it will be a long time before we have this opportunity. Captain Nemo knows we may try to escape. All he needs to do is keep the *Nautilus* in the open sea, and watch us closely when we are near land.'

'Well, we shall see. Anyway, please be ready to leave at a moment's notice.'

With these words, Ned left us, probably to cook some more food which we could take with us.

The volcano

Poor Ned! He spent the next few days in a most excited state. Most of the time he was in the sitting-room, looking at the position of the *Nautilus* on the charts, and at the instruments which told us her speed and depth. Whenever the ship was on the surface, he was up on the platform working out our position for himself. Whenever the doors in the sitting-room wall were open, he looked out to see if we were near any island not marked on the maps.

For the first few days, our course made him very hopeful. We sailed through the islands of the Aegean Sea, and Ned was sure we would have a chance of escaping. But the opportunity never came. The *Nautilus* sailed mostly at 900 feet below the surface, so even in the boat, we could never reach the top without diving suits.

On one occasion we sailed right up to an under-water volcano. This was close to the island of Santorini, where, as it is well known, small islands have appeared in the sea and disappeared again.

The first sign that we were near this volcano was that the temperature in the ship became uncomfortably hot. I was forced to take off my jacket. Captain Nemo came in.

'Feeling hot, I see, Professor,' he said.

'Yes, I am. What is happening? If the ship gets any hotter we shan't be able to bear it.'

'Look at the sea,' he said.

The doors slid open, and to my astonishment the water was entirely white all around us. Bubbles of gas passed up through the water, which seemed to be boiling. I touched the window, but quickly took my hand back, because it was so hot. As the *Nautilus* sailed slowly on, the water turned red.

'Captain!' I shouted. 'The ship will melt. We must go back.'

'Yes,' he said. 'It would be a little unwise to go on.'

He gave orders for the ship to change course. We left the boiling water behind us. Gradually the temperature inside the *Nautilus* went down. After a few miles, we returned to the surface, and obtained a new supply of air. Then at last the strange chemical smell that had spread throughout the vessel gradually disappeared. I was extremely glad that Ned had not decided to leave the Nautilus while we were near to that island. We might well have escaped, but we should certainly not have enjoyed our freedom for long.

We sailed on, westwards, between Crete and Greece. In the late afternoon, Captain Nemo came down into the sitting-room and looked through the window.

As usual, I was noting the different types of fish that I saw. Suddenly, amongst the fish, I saw a human body. It was not dead but alive. It was a man swimming.

'A shipwrecked sailor!' I cried to
5   Captain Nemo. 'We must save him!'

Captain Nemo said nothing.
The man came up to the glass
window and looked in. I looked at Captain Nemo, and was astonished to see him make a sign with his hand. The
10   swimmer raised his hand in reply and swam away.

'That was Nicholas Pesca,' Captain Nemo explained. 'He is a famous diver and swimmer who spends more of his life in the sea than on land. He often swims from one island to another, and can even swim from the Greek
15   mainland to Crete.'

'Do you know him, Captain?' I asked.
'I do,' he replied.

The box of gold

He said nothing more, but went towards a piece of furniture which was standing in a corner of the room. Beside it I saw a strong box bound with iron. On the cover was a copper plate bearing the letter 'N'.

Captain Nemo then opened the piece of furniture, which was a sort of cupboard. Inside it were a great many bars of gold. I watched him in amazement as he took out the bars of gold and packed them carefully in a box. I judged the gold to be worth at least five million dollars. Then he shut the box, locked it, and wrote an address on the lid.

When he had done this, he pressed a bell. Some members of the crew came in. They pushed the box out of the room, and left Captain Nemo and me looking at each other.

'Did you say anything, Professor?' he asked.

'No, ah, no, I said nothing,' I said nervously.

'Then I will wish you goodnight,' he said, and he left me alone.

Where had he obtained so much gold? What was he going to do with it? I suddenly remembered the rebellion that had taken place on the island of Crete, where the inhabitants were fighting for their freedom from the Turks, who ruled the island with great cruelty. Was the diver connected in any way with these people? Was Captain Nemo helping them?

I longed to ask Captain Nemo himself, but I did not dare. If he had wanted to tell me, he could easily have done so. He was not the sort of person I felt I could ask questions of. He was so large and strong, that I felt very weak compared to him, and his eyes made me even more afraid. They seemed to look straight through me.

I went to bed and fell asleep thinking about these things. But I was soon woken up. I felt the movement of the boat, and knew that the Nautilus was on the surface again. Then I heard footsteps climbing up the staircase, onto the platform. I expected that they would unfasten the boat, and they did. There was the sound of many men coming and going. Then all noise stopped. About two hours later, the same noises were repeated. The boat was fixed to the *Nautilus* again, and the men came back down the staircase.

Next morning, Ned and Conseil came to my cabin. Ned asked me what had been going on.

'I was hoping that we might be able to get away, for Crete was not far off,' he said. 'But the sailors were working all through the night. I did not dare leave our cabin.'

I told him about what I had seen. 'I think that someone has now got the gold, perhaps the Cretans who were rebelling against the Turks last year,' I said.

'I suppose that is possible. If so, we are beginning to uncover Captain Nemo's secrets,' said Conseil. 'When he rescued the Indian diver, he said he tried to help the victims of an unjust government. Perhaps he goes around the world giving help to any people who are trying to win their freedom.'

'That seems very possible, Conseil. Perhaps Captain Nemo is working for freedom. But where does he get his gold from? And what were we not allowed to see in the Timor Sea? And what is his real name?'

'Working for freedom!' said Ned. 'What about our freedom? I don't care who he is, as long as I can get away from him. It doesn't look as if we shall get a chance in the Mediterranean, if we stay in the open sea like this.'

A TREASURE FLEET

An opportunity to escape

Ned was quite right. We had no chance at all of escaping in the Mediterranean, for we travelled straight through it at a steady speed of twenty-five knots. Captain Nemo chose the most direct course. Ned felt that he was doing 5 this on purpose, to prevent our escaping. I rather thought the same. The sliding doors were seldom opened, and we could see very little of the underwater life in that famous sea.

When we had passed the Straits of Gibraltar, the 10 *Nautilus* sailed up the coast of Portugal.

'You see, Ned,' I said to him as we examined the charts, 'we'll have plenty of opportunity to escape once the *Nautilus* reaches the northern seas of Europe.'

'We must try tonight.' 15

'Tonight!' I exclaimed.

'Yes, sir, tonight. You promised me that we should make an attempt as soon as we had a chance. Now we have a chance. Tonight we shall be quite near the Portuguese coast. The weather is fine and there is no moon. There is 20 a fair south-west wind, which will blow us quickly to land. We must try tonight.'

I must have looked sad, for Ned went on, 'Tonight at 9.00 p.m., Professor. I have already told Conseil. At that time Captain Nemo will be shut up in his room, probably 25 in bed. None of the crew will see us. Conseil and I will go to the central staircase, while you, Professor Arronax, will remain in the library, waiting for my signal. The oars, the mast, and the sail are in the boat. I have collected enough food, and obtained some tools with which to 30 unfasten the boat from the *Nautilus*. So all is ready.'

'But the sea is rough.'

'I agree, but we must risk that. Freedom is worth a little danger. Anyway, the boat is strong, and the wind will quickly blow us to shore. By this time tomorrow we may be 200 miles away, and with luck we shall have reached land. We will meet again tonight.'

With these words he left me alone. I was most unhappy, for I did not want to leave the ship. I had hoped to see so much more. Although I never felt comfortable in Captain Nemo's presence, I trusted him more than Ned did. I was sure that one day he would allow us to leave his ship, and tell the world about our discoveries.

I thought of breaking my promise and refusing to join Ned. I was certain Conseil would stay with me. But that would be most unfair to Ned, because he saved our lives after we fell overboard from the *Abraham Lincoln*. Besides that, I had to think about Conseil, who was my servant and would do anything I asked. Also, I could not be certain that Captain Nemo would allow us to leave, or that there would be another opportunity like the present one. Finally, I remembered how we had run onto the rocks in the Torres Straits, and I knew that what Ned had said about danger was quite true. There might be another accident like that, from which we would not escape.

Anxious moments

So, with a sad heart, I collected my notes, arranged them in order, and tied them together in a bundle. I laid out the clothes that I would wear, and returned to the sitting-room. Here I spent the afternoon looking at the specimens in the glass cases. Every now and then I looked at the compass, to see if the *Nautilus* was sailing away from the Portuguese coast, but our course did not change.

I wondered what Captain Nemo would think. He could not blame us, for we had not promised to stay on board.

However, he had saved our lives and made our time on
board most comfortable and most interesting. It seemed
bad manners to leave him without saying goodbye. But I
could hardly do that without letting him know about our
plans. Anyway, I had not seen him since I watched him   5
pack up the gold.

As the hours went by, I began to get more and more
nervous. I was especially afraid of being caught by
Captain Nemo, and of what he might do to us. I was also
a little anxious in case we ran into difficulties. I could not   10
forget that the last time I had been on the open sea I had
nearly drowned.

My dinner was served as usual at 7.00 p.m., and I tried
to eat, but could not manage more than a few mouthfuls.
There were two hours to go before we started. I walked   15
into the sitting-room and then into the dining-room, and
then into the library, taking a last look at the treasures I
had come to know so well.

Eventually it was time to dress, and collect my packet
of notes. When we first joined the ship, we had been given   20
thick, warm clothing. I now put on my sealskin coat and
my sea boots. As soon as I was ready, I left my cabin.
There was no sound except the noise made by the
engines. I went to the sitting-room and waited there for
Ned's signal.   25

After a few moments of waiting, the noise from the
engines grew less. Then it stopped altogether. There was
a slight bump. The ship was resting on the bottom of the
sea. I was worried. Nine o'clock passed and Ned's signal
did not come. I decided to go out and tell Ned that we   30
should give up the attempt, since we would easily be
heard.

Then Captain Nemo came into the room. He appeared
not to notice my nervousness. He must have seen my
clothes, but he made no comment about them. Instead he   35
said, 'Ah, Professor, I have been looking for you. I want
to show you something.'

Treasure ships

The sliding doors opened and I saw an amazing sight. For a mile round the *Nautilus* the waters were lit up by the ship's electric light. The sandy floor of the ocean was clean and bright. Some of the ship's crew, in their diving suits, were clearing away half rotten barrels and cases, from the middle of the wrecks of a dozen old sailing ships. Out of these barrels and cases had fallen bars of silver and gold, and piles of gold coins and jewels. The men were gathering these treasures up, loading them into new boxes, and bringing them into the *Nautilus*.

'You are looking at Spanish treasure ships, Professor. They were sent from the Spanish lands in America to help the French and Spanish in their war against Austria, Holland and England. They were caught by the English fleet here at Vigo Bay in 1702. Rather than allow them to be captured, the commander ordered his men to burn the ships and sink them.'

'And now you have found them and are taking the treasure.'

'Yes, from here and from a thousand other spots where I have found wrecked treasure ships.'

'But there are several groups of people trying to rescue this treasure from the sea. The money they spend will be wasted, because when they find the ships, there will be no treasure left. I am not sorry for them, but I am sorry that this treasure will never be put to any good use.'

'Never be put to any good use!' roared Captain Nemo. 'Do you think, sir, that all this treasure is useless because I have it? Do you think that I am collecting it for myself alone? Do you think that I don't know there are millions of people in the world who are treated unjustly by their rulers? Did I not tell you that I was once treated unjustly myself, and am now trying to help them?'

Captain Nemo said no more. Perhaps he wished he had not said so much. He went away to see that the treasure was being collected correctly, and I returned to my room, which I had not expected to see again.

We now had one more answer to our questions about Captain Nemo. He obtained his gold and silver from wrecked treasure ships. And this treasure he then gave to people and societies that were struggling for justice and freedom.

But we were not free. We had chosen to escape on the very night when the crew would be up and hard at work.

Into the Atlantic

Next morning I discovered that Ned and Conseil had never left their cabin.

'Do you know what was going on, sir?' Conseil asked me, when we met as usual in the sitting-room.

'Captain Nemo was collecting treasure from a Spanish treasure fleet that was sunk in 1702,' I said, and I told them in detail what I had seen.

'I wish I had been out there filling a bag with coins and jewels for myself,' said Ned. 'We have been prevented from escaping this time, but all is not lost. In which direction are we sailing now?'

We looked at the compass. It read south-south-west. We were leaving Europe behind us. When the *Nautilus* rose to the surface to fill its tanks with fresh air, we rushed to the platform, but could not see any land. There was nothing but a vast sea. At 12.00 p.m. the ship's position was marked on the charts. It showed that we were 150 miles from the nearest land, and moving south into the Atlantic.

Ned was filled with rage and disappointment. There was nothing I could do to calm him, and he soon went off by himself to recover his temper. As for myself, I was very pleased, for it seemed that, after all, I should see the wonders of the Atlantic. But on many occasions during the next few months, I found myself wishing we had been able to escape, when we were so close to the shores of Portugal.

The *Nautilus* continued to sail towards the south. Either we would sail round Cape Horn to the Pacific Ocean, and so complete our journey around the world, or we would sail further and further south, towards the South Pole.

I thought it very unlikely that Captain Nemo would try to sail to the South Pole. Nobody had so far managed to reach either the South Pole or the North Pole. More important, it was nearly 21st March. That day marks the end of summer at the South Pole, and the beginning of six months of darkness and dreadful cold. If we tried to reach the South Pole, and were delayed in any way, we would run the risk of being frozen to death in continual night.

Captain Nemo, however, did decide to try and reach the South Pole. So that the record of this journey may be absolutely clear, I will write it in the form of a diary, and I will note our position at 6.00 a.m. each day.

14th March: 2,000 miles from the South Pole

We saw floating ice for the first time. The pieces of ice were between twenty and twenty-five yards long. We stayed up on the platform, and could see on the horizon the shining white light which whale-hunters call 'ice blink'.

In the afternoon we saw icebergs for the first time. Ned had often seen them before, but Conseil and I were amazed by their size, their steep sides, and the bright colours that flashed in the sunlight.

We passed the South Orkney Islands and the New Shetland Islands. They were once inhabited by thousands of seals, but these were all killed off by the fishermen from Europe. Instead of noise and life, there was silence and death on these islands.

15th March: 1,400 miles from the South Pole

There was now so much ice that it was very difficult to find clear water. Captain Nemo, however, seemed to have experience of these conditions, for he was able to guide the ship very accurately.

It was becoming very cold. We were kept warm by our clothes, which were made of seal fur. Inside the *Nautilus* the electric power kept everything at a steady, comfortable temperature.

16th March: 1,100 miles from the South Pole

Early that morning, the *Nautilus* came to a stop for the first time, because of the ice. Surrounded by ice on all sides, she could not move forwards. The ice was not too thick, however. It was possible for the *Nautilus* to move back a little way, go forwards again at full speed, and smash into it. This was most exciting to watch from the platform. The ice was thrown up in the air and fell down all round us. Sometimes the ship forced a channel through the ice. Sometimes it climbed up onto the ice, and broke it by its weight. Sometimes it went below the ice, and broke it by lifting the ice up from below.

We made much less progress. It often took us a long time to break through a barrier of ice. In addition, it snowed heavily, and thick fog in the afternoon made it impossible to see very far ahead. Every now and again we had to spend time clearing ice away from the platform. We wondered how soon it would be before we would have to turn back.

17th March: 1,000 miles from the South Pole

At 4.00 a.m. we were finally stuck, and could go no further. We had tried to hit the ice in front of us several times, but the ice formed so quickly behind us, that we were soon entirely shut in by frozen water.

The cloud lifted, and we saw a most wonderful sight. In front of us we could see a solid line of ice stretching into the distance. Blocks of ice formed strange shapes, which shone in the sunlight in many brilliant colours. I was certain we could go no further, and I was very worried in case we could not go back.

Captain Nemo then announced his plan. This was to sink some 2,000 feet below the surface, and at that depth to continue our voyage south, under the ice barrier. He argued that the ice was only floating on an open sea. It was not more than 300 feet high, and although three-quarters of a lump of ice is below the surface, the lowest depths of ice would not be more than 900 feet. If we went below that depth, we would be safe. The distance to the Pole was then 1,000 miles. If we travelled at our usual speed of twenty-five knots, we should reach it in about forty hours.

One of three things might happen. The best was that we should find open sea ahead of us near the Pole. Then we would have no difficulty in filling the ship with fresh air, and making the return journey under the ice.

The second possibility was that we would find our way blocked by land. If that happened, we would have to return. There was enough air on the ship to last us four days. In addition, there was the air in the reserve tanks and the oxygen bottles.

The third possibility was that we would reach the area of the South Pole, and find the ice too thick to break through. In this case we would have to return, and would find ourselves very short of air. But if we were careful we could last five days.

We agreed very willingly to the plan. If we had any doubts about our success, we did not mention them. No one suggested that we might have an accident. We all had complete confidence in Captain Nemo. Our preparations were made. The tanks were filled with air, and the ice that had formed round the ship was broken up. At 12.00 p.m. we descended into the depths. We passed the bottom of the ice at 900 feet, and dropped down another 1,000 feet. Then we sailed steadily and without difficulty towards the south.

TRAPPED

18th March: 600 miles from the South Pole

All day we travelled under the ice. We felt very cheerful as we felt the expedition would be successful.

In the evening we began to test the thickness of the
5 ice. Our speed was reduced and the ship went upwards. The ice was 1,000 feet thick at the first spot we tried, a good deal thicker than at the edge.

Three times that night the *Nautilus* tried again. Each time she met solid ice, but the thickness gradually grew less.

10 ### 19th March: 100 miles from the South Pole

Every hour the *Nautilus* tested the ceiling of ice above it. We all became most excited, and never left the sitting-room, so that we could watch the instruments all the time. At 10.00 a.m. the captain announced that we were in the
15 open sea once more. The hatches were opened, and we stepped out onto the platform into the open air. Pieces of ice floated on the water, and not far away there was a coastline.

The success of our journey now depended on where
20 we were. Captain Nemo had made as careful a measurement as possible of the distance and direction in which we had travelled. He calculated that we were very near the South Pole. But we needed the sun to rise so that we could calculate our position accurately. Unfortunately
25 thick cloud covered the sky.

We sailed towards the land, and anchored very close to it. The crew put the boat into the water, and Captain Nemo rowed Conseil and myself to the shore. Ned was not with us. He was so angry at not being able to escape, that he
30 did not want to be anywhere near the captain.

Conseil was about to jump out onto the beach, but I held him back, so that the captain could be the first man ever to step on the South Pole. Captain Nemo thanked me and said, 'I once made a promise never to step on land again. But this land is different. No man has ever stepped on it before.'

Saying this, he jumped out of the boat and stepped on to a rock. He held out his hands towards the land and stood there for five minutes, as if taking possession of it.

When we joined him, we made our way to some high ground, and set up the instruments for taking the position of the sun. Unfortunately the clouds were too thick, and we had to return to the ship and wait till the following day.

20th March: Near the South Pole

In the morning Conseil and I made a journey by ourselves. Four sailors rowed us over in the boat. We walked two miles along the coast, looking carefully at the wild life and plants there. There were thousands of penguins and an equally large number of seals. Further on, we saw a few elephant seals which were an enormous size.

On our return, we found that Captain Nemo had come ashore and was hoping to see the sun, so that he could fix our position. We waited till midday, but still the clouds did not break up, and we could not calculate the angle of the sun.

21st March: Near the South Pole

This was the last day on which we would be able to see the sun at this point. For the next six months the sun would never appear, and it would be continual night. If the sun did appear, it would be an easy task to judge our position. If we were at the South Pole as we hoped, the sun would be cut exactly in half by the horizon.

This time Captain Nemo decided to sail a little further along the coast. From here, we climbed a steep hill about 500 yards high, and at the top he set up his instruments and waited. A strong wind was blowing, and after some time the clouds began to break up. By 11.00 a.m. the sky above us was clear, but there was still cloud on the horizon. At last, even that cloud began to blow away, and by noon the sky was completely clear. At that very moment the sun rose. The top half of the circle of the sun appeared above the horizon. There was no doubt. We were at the South Pole.

Captain Nemo opened up a black flag which had a large gold 'N' in the centre. He stuck it in the ground and said, 'I, Captain Nemo, on this day, 21st March 1868, am the first to set foot on the South Pole. I now take possession of all this land.'

Captain Nemo was already the ruler of the seas and oceans. Now he was the ruler of some land as well. No one could attack him, because he was the only man in the world who could reach the ocean floor or the South Pole. The captain of the *Nautilus* ruled most of the planet Earth.

I wondered what he would do now. There were still parts of the ocean that we had not visited, but we still had the treasure from Vigo Bay on board. I expected that the captain would want to take it to groups of people who were fighting for their freedom.

But first he had to get away from the South Pole. We had to do this quickly because the open sea would freeze up quickly, and the ice barrier would soon get deeper in the long winter night.

We filled up every section of the ship with fresh air, and checked that all the metal bottles were full of oxygen under pressure.

22nd March: At the South Pole

By the early hours of the morning, we were ready to leave. The *Nautilus* sank 1,000 feet below the surface, and then sailed north at a steady speed of twenty-five knots. We made good progress all day, and expected to reach open sea again early on the morning of the 24th.

23rd March: 500 miles north

At 3.00 a.m. I was woken up by a violent shock. I sat up in my bed and listened in the darkness. Then there was another shock, and I was thrown out of bed. I felt my way to the door and went into the sitting-room. It was difficult to walk, for though there was some light from the electric bulbs, the ship was at an angle and the furniture thrown all around. The *Nautilus* was on its side and not moving at all.

Conseil and Ned also made their way to the sitting-room, and we tried to understand what had happened. I thought that we must have come up to the surface and got stuck in the ice. But the instruments showed that we were still more than 1,000 feet under. We went in search of Captain Nemo to find out what had happened. He was calm, but it was clear from his face that he was very worried.

An iceberg had turned over in the water. This can happen when the part under the sea melts, and the top becomes heavier by the addition of snow. The first shock was caused by this iceberg striking the ship as it sank down. The second shock was caused by the same iceberg as it floated back up again. At present the ship was being lifted to the surface by this ice. Our safety depended on whether there was open sea above us or more ice. If there was ice, we should be crushed between two surfaces.

By great good fortune, there was open sea above us. After a short time, we stopped moving up and the ship returned to an even keel. With a great feeling of thankfulness we rushed up onto the platform. But we were not free. The sky was hidden from us by a roof of ice, which was only three feet above our heads. We were in a tunnel that had been made when the iceberg broke off. We now had to find a way out.

All that day Captain Nemo tried to find a passage that would enable us to get below the ice barrier again. There was no room to turn the ship. Initially Captain Nemo went ahead, but soon came to the end of the tunnel. We had to turn back.

We found a narrow passage that opened up and led down under the surface. The ship sank in it to a depth of 900 feet. We seemed to have found a passage between the iceberg and the barrier. Our confidence returned, and we waited for the moment when we would be free once more.

The tunnel then grew narrower. The ship had to go more and more slowly till we were hardly moving at all. At exactly 8.25 a.m. there was a third shock. The iceberg had moved again, and trapped us.

We now had to face the possibility of a slow death. We had plenty of food and water, but we would soon be short of air. Captain Nemo calculated that we had enough in the ship to last for three days. After that, we would have to depend on the air in the reserve tanks, and in the oxygen bottles. They might keep us alive for another two days at the most. After that, we would slowly die — unless we could get out.

The iceberg might move again, but we could not depend on it. Our only chance was to get outside the ship, and find out how thick the ice was. Captain Nemo led out some of his crew, dressed in diving suits and wearing breathing equipment. After about two hours he returned *5* to make his report.

He had not tried to test the roof. There was no point in trying to go up again. He had tested all the sides, but there was still ice after fourty-five feet. The only chance of escape was through the floor, which seemed to be thirty *10* feet thick. Somehow we had to dig a ditch in the ice, wide enough and long enough to let the ship through.

By 6.00 p.m. the first group of men were ready for action. Every person on board was put into a group and equipped with special tools. The work was very hard and *15* uncomfortable, and it was not possible to keep going for longer than two hours. So every two hours a fresh group took over. Ned Land worked as hard as any of us, and was certainly more useful than either Conseil or myself, for we were not used to this sort of work. But Captain *20* Nemo set a fine example to us all, working faster, and with more energy, than any of us, passengers or crew.

24th March: 500 miles north

By 6.00 a.m. we had cut away the first block of ice. It was a huge amount of ice, about 600 cubic yards, but it was only three feet deep. It had taken us twelve hours to dig it out and there were still twenty-seven feet left. That meant it would take us four and a half days to get free.

We only had enough air for four days. Even worse, there were still 500 miles to go under the ice barrier before we would reach the open sea. That would take us another day.

All day the groups worked, and by the evening we had dug out another three feet, and were starting on the seventh.

25th March: 500 miles north

This day was spent in exactly the same way as the day before. By now the air in the ship was beginning to smell bad. This meant that it was a pleasure to use the bottles of pure air, which those digging in the ice carried. Although the work was difficult and tiring, and although our hands became sore and our muscles ached, we looked forward to the moment when we could put on our diving suits and start work again.

During one of the times I was outside, I pointed out to Captain Nemo a most serious change. The water in the tunnel in which we were trapped was steadily freezing. It was clear that the walls were getting thicker, and that before long they would close in on the ship. Captain Nemo had also noticed this, but had not yet thought of any solution to the problem. We would simply have to work even harder.

26th March: 500 miles north

Twelve feet of ice had been lifted by that morning, but eighteen remained. The air in the ship was now finished, and we were using up the reserves in the tanks. Life on board was becoming very uncomfortable. We moved around as little as possible, so as not to use up more air than we had to.

By now the freezing up of the walls was making the task of digging more difficult. Not only that, but they seemed to be freezing up faster as the space got smaller.

Two solutions occurred to Captain Nemo. One was to let all the water freeze. Since ice occupies a larger space than water, the pressure of the ice would be very great, and might break the walls and free us without our having to dig any more. The danger would be that the *Nautilus* herself might not be able to stand the pressure, and so be damaged before the walls cracked.

The other possibility was to use the engines of the *Nautilus* to boil water, and so raise the temperature of the water outside enough to prevent it from freezing. This was what Captain Nemo decided to do. The temperature of the water was raised in three hours by two degrees, and in the next two hours by a further four degrees. During the night the process continued, and the temperature rose to thirty-four degrees. We were not able to make the temperature rise any higher but this was enough, since ice forms at thirty-two degrees.

27th March: 500 miles north

By the morning of the fourth day, we had cleared eighteen feet of ice from the floor of the cave. Twelve feet remained to go.

Those who were outside worked harder and faster than ever before. Better progress could be made because the water was no longer freezing in the trench. Also, each group worked for four hours instead of two, which saved time. Muscles ached, and there were some injuries, but nobody did less work. That day six feet were dug out. Six were left.

The work outside was hard but, inside the ship, life was very miserable. Simply lying on a bed was very painful. My head ached and my eyes felt very heavy. It was easy to fall asleep, but then I would wake up gasping for breath, with a bitter taste in my mouth. All of us were affected in the same way, but somehow Conseil managed to look after me as well as himself.

28th March: 500 miles north

The work had gone on through the night and by 6.00 a.m. there remained just three feet to dig. But the condition of the air inside the ship was so poor, that it looked as if we should get free too late. For when we had dug through the last piece of ice, we still had to sail for at least a day until we reached the open sea again.

Fortunately Captain Nemo decided to try using the weight of the ship to break through the ice. Holes were cut through the ice floor to make it weaker. Then the position of the *Nautilus* was changed, so that it rested in the ditch we had dug. The reserve tanks were filled with water, so that its weight was greatly increased. We waited. It was our last chance. No one spoke.

Then we heard the sound of ice cracking. Very, very slowly, the ship began to sink. We were free.

Captain Nemo set our course to the north, and the engines worked at full speed. Those who had work to do on board used the remaining bottles of oxygen. The rest of us lay still. Our faces were purple, our lips were blue, and we could neither think, nor speak, nor move. The pain was terrible. Our lungs hurt from trying to breathe the bad air, and our heads ached.

Meanwhile the *Nautilus* sailed on at the frightening speed of fifty knots. After about five hours, Captain Nemo began to test the thickness of the ice. It proved to be no more than sixty feet thick. He could wait no longer. He threw the ship at full speed against the ice ceiling. Several times he took the ship back, and then went forward again and hit the same spot. Each time the ship struck the ice, we felt a shock.

At last the steel sword of the ship broke right through the ice. The ship shot up into the open air and fell onto the ice, which broke up under its weight. The sailors tore open the hatches, and pure air flowed into all parts of the ship. We breathed again.

THE BATTLE OF THE OCTOPUSES

The monster at the window

The *Nautilus* came out from under the ice on 28th March. She then sailed steadily north towards Cape Horn, the southern tip of South America. We did not know whether Captain Nemo would sail west into the Pacific, and so complete with us an underwater journey round the world, or whether he would return to the Atlantic. As it happened, he chose to sail into the Atlantic, and we moved up towards the east coast of South America.

When we reached Cape Horn on 31st March, we had travelled about 17,000 leagues, or 50,000 miles, under the sea with the *Nautilus*. By 16th April we had gone another 4,000 miles and could see some of the islands of the West Indies in the distance.

Our speed and direction, therefore, were steady. The three of us were pleased that our course was taking us towards home. Ned was as determined as ever to leave the ship. Our narrow escape under the ice had made him even more certain that we were in great danger of losing our lives as well as our freedom. Conseil and I also began to look forward to leaving the *Nautilus*.

There were still plenty of strange creatures to study, and a great deal to write, but as the days went by, I began to reach the end of the books I was writing. I became worried that they might be held prisoner like me, and never be published. In addition, it seemed unlikely that there would be any more great wonders to see. Finally, our adventure at the South Pole had made us feel content with what we had already seen and done. We did not want to travel any further with Captain Nemo.

As for the captain, we never saw him. Before our polar visit, he had been ready to comment on my book and notes by adding words and sentences in pencil. While we were sailing to the South Pole, he had been very willing to talk, and we had felt quite safe. But after we came out of the ice, he did not come near us. This separation made us feel more worried about his intentions towards us, and so we thought we should escape when we could.

There was, however, one event in which he showed his old energy and friendliness towards us. But it was an event that I remember with horror and disgust, for it was something more terrible than anything else that happened to us.

We were quite near the Bahamas. The sliding doors in the sitting-room were open, and we were looking at the underwater rocks, which were covered with seaweed and strange-looking crabs and shellfish.

'That looks the sort of place where you might find an octopus,' I said. 'I have heard that they like to live in the cracks of rocks, and there is plenty for them to feed on here.'

'What are they?' asked Ned. 'I have never seen one.'

'They have eight arms or legs which come out from their heads. They have no body.'

'How big are they?'

'Oh, they vary in size. Some are quite small, and are eaten by some people, who think them delicious. Others are very big.'

'How big?' asked Ned again.

'I have seen one octopus that was so big that it was able to drag a ship down into the water with only one arm,' said Conseil.

'I don't believe you,' said Ned. 'Where?'

'In a church,' Conseil replied.

'What do you mean? How can a ship or an octopus get into a church?'

'It was in a picture,' said Conseil.

'Oh, a picture! That is not real.'

'I have heard of that picture and of that story,' I said. 'There are other stories too, of people building a church on a rock. When they had finished, the rock moved into the sea. It was really an octopus.'   5

'But surely you scientists don't believe in such stories?' said Ned in astonishment.

'These stories are interesting, and there is evidence to show that very large octopuses do exist. The bones of the head of one octopus in a museum in France are two yards   10 long. Some scientists say that the arms of such a creature would be nine yards long. As recently as 1861, some fishermen tried to catch one of these monsters in the Indian Ocean. They could not kill it, but managed to cut off an arm. Scientists have measured this arm, and have   15 calculated the size of the whole animal.'

'Was its head about six yards long?' asked Conseil, who had returned to the window.

'Yes, it was.'

'Were its eyes at the back, and did they stick out?'   20

'Yes, that is right. All octopuses are like that.'

'And were its eight arms some twenty yards long, and very thick and strong?'

'Yes, that is what they said.'

'Then come and look at it, for it is outside looking at   25 us.'

Not a pleasant sight

We leapt to our feet and rushed to the window. We were thankful that glass protected us from the monster that we saw. It was just as Conseil had described, with a mouth   30 formed like the beak of a bird. The teeth inside were very sharp, and the beak itself looked very sharp at the edges.

About five other creatures of the same type joined this one. They tore at the ship with their beaks and tried to pull it to pieces with their arms, but of course the iron   35 body of the ship was too strong for them. The *Nautilus* increased its speed, but it could not get away from the octopuses. They were just as fast.

Suddenly the ship stopped.

'Have we hit anything?' I asked.

'If we have, at least we are not caught under ice or a rock. We shall be able to float to the surface,' said Conseil.

The ship began to rise in the water. Captain Nemo came in and looked through the window. We waited for him to speak.

'They are not a very pleasant sight,' he said at length. 'Very soon we shall have to fight with them, man against beast.'

'Why? What has happened?' I asked.

'One of them has got its arms wrapped round the rudder and the propeller. We cannot move. That means that we must drive away all these monsters, and then go under the ship to remove the one that has got tied up.'

'That should be quite easy with our electric bullets,' Conseil said.

'I am afraid not,' replied the captain. 'The bullets will have no effect on such soft bodies. The only way to fight them is with axes.'

'And harpoons,' said Ned. 'I should like to show you what a harpoon can do.'

'I shall be glad of your help,' the captain replied in a solemn voice.

'We shall come as well,' I said.

We went out to the staircase. About ten men with axes were already there. Conseil and I took up an axe each. Ned held his harpoon.

The *Nautilus* had by now risen to the surface. One of the sailors who was standing at the top of the staircase opened up the hatches. As soon as the screws were loosened, the hatches were torn away with great violence. One of the beasts must have been pulling at it with its arms.

At once, one of these arms slid in through the opening, and came down the stairs towards us. Twenty others appeared in the opening above it.

An octopus kills a sailor

Captain Nemo cut the arm of the octopus with his axe, and the broken piece fell heavily to the floor beside us. Then we all moved up the stairs, eager to reach the platform where we would have room to fight. Two more arms came down towards us. One of them seized the man in front of Captain Nemo, and lifted him up with enormous power. Captain Nemo gave a loud shout and rushed up the last steps. We hurried after him.

What a scene we saw when we got outside! The unlucky man was high above us, held up by several arms which were wrapped round him. He screamed in pain and fear. I heard the words, 'Help! Help!' spoken in French, which made me even more eager to help. We attacked the octopus that was holding him. We stabbed at it with our knives. The rest of the crew fought the other monsters and prevented them from reaching the wounded man.

At one moment it seemed that we would save him, for we managed to cut off seven of the monster's eight arms. We had almost struck off the eighth when the creature spat out a stream of black liquid. We were blinded by it.
5 When we had wiped the liquid from our eyes, the octopus had gone, taking the unlucky sailor with it.

At once we joined the rest of the crew as they fought the other monsters. Ten or twelve of these disgusting creatures climbed up onto the hull of the ship and moved
10 towards the platform. Many arms were cut off by our axes. Many eyes were blinded, and heads broken, by Ned's harpoon.

Then Ned fell down. He slipped and rolled over, underneath an octopus that had climbed up onto the hull.
15 It held Ned tightly between two arms and raised its beak to strike. I rushed to help him, but Captain Nemo was there before me. He drove his axe between the jaws of the monster. Its arms loosened their hold, and Ned freed himself. Rising to his feet, he forced his harpoon deep into
20 the monster's heart.

'My turn to save you,' said Captain Nemo.

Ned bowed his head in reply. He said nothing, for he hated Captain Nemo too much, even though this was the second time the captain had saved his life, and he had
25 saved the captain from the shark.

The struggle lasted fifteen minutes. In the end the octopuses left. Many arms, and much blood and dirt lay on the ship, and on the platform. Two men dived under the ship, and freed the rudder and the propeller. All the
30 crew were safe, except for the poor man who had been dragged down into the sea.

A terrible storm

35 I felt great pity for the sailor who had died, since he was a Frenchman. In his great fear he had cried out two words of French, instead of the special language of the *Nautilus*.

I wondered if there were any other Frenchmen on board, and if they would help us if we needed them.

Captain Nemo felt even more deeply about it. We saw him from time to time, but he never spoke to us. He spent many hours looking out over the waves as though he hoped somehow to see the dead man, but of course he never did. Ned said that he saw him weeping. While he was suffering from sorrow, he gave no orders to the crew. We sailed about over the same spot for ten days. It was not until 1st May that the ship again moved north.

By now we were very eager to leave the ship. We were not very far from the coast of the United States, and we hoped there would be a good opportunity to escape. As the ship went slowly north past Cape Hatterall, and towards New York, we became very hopeful.

We had two advantages at that time. The boat went slowly and stayed on the surface. Also, nobody on board seemed to bother about us. Unfortunately the weather was so bad that it would have been very unwise to try to leave the ship.

When we were a few miles off New York, we went through a terrible storm. Instead of diving under the waves into the calm water below, Captain Nemo chose to stay on the surface. Not only were we very uncomfortable because the ship moved about so much, but also much of the furniture, and many of the boxes of specimens were thrown about and damaged.

This was strange behaviour on the part of Captain Nemo, and it became even stranger. As the storm began, he tied himself firmly to the rail round the platform and stayed there alone, all through the wind, rain, thunder and lightning.

Either he wanted to punish himself for the death of his companion, or else he hoped to die. Several times waves crashed right over the ship, and several times lightning struck the steel point as the ship rose up over the waves.

5 There was no danger to the ship. It was strong enough to sail through the roughest seas, and we were far enough from land not to be driven onto any rocks. But it was terrifying to know that the captain might be killed at any moment, and that he was not controlling the ship in any
10 way. It was only when the storm had passed that he untied himself and came down to the sitting-room. Here he gave orders for the ship to descend, and we sailed in calm water once again.

Is the captain mad?

15 The three of us met to discuss what had happened. As usual, Ned was the most eager for action, and now Conseil and I agreed with him completely.

'Professor, we must do something quickly, or we may be killed by the mad actions of this captain.'

20 'I agree, Ned, but what do you suggest? Every time we plan to escape, something prevents us. Either the crew are up all night, or the weather is so bad that we cannot risk it.'

'I think that you should ask Captain Nemo to let us go,'
25 said Ned.

'But you know what he'll say,' I said.

'I know that he has said that we may never leave the ship. But he may change his mind. We know that we must take any risk to save our lives. If he says no, then we are
30 no worse off. If he says yes, then we need not take any risk.'

'Ned is right, sir,' said Conseil. 'We lose nothing if you speak with him.'

I agreed to try, though I was sure it would be no use.
35 First I had to find him. He was in his own room, bending

over maps and charts. I knocked on the door, which was
slightly open, but he did not answer. I went in and stood
beside him. He looked up.

'What do you want?' he said roughly.

'To speak to you, sir,' I replied. 5

'But I am busy, Professor. I am working. I leave you
alone. Why can't you leave me alone?'

This was not a good start to our conversation, but I did
not go away.

'Sir,' I said in a firm voice, 'I must talk to you about a 10
very important matter.'

'What is that? Have you noticed something that I
haven't? Has the sea shown you any new secrets? I don't
expect so. Look at this, Professor. Here is my book, written
in several languages. In it I have written a full account of 15
all that I have discovered in the sea. When I have finished
it, I will sign it. I will put the book and the full story of
my life in a box that will not let water in, and will never
sink. The last person alive on board this ship will throw
the box into the sea, and the waves will carry it wherever 20
they like.'

So one day we shall know his name, I thought, and we
shall read his own history.

I ask for our freedom

'I am very glad that you are writing these books, Captain,' 25
I said. 'It is most important that you tell your discoveries
to the world. But I feel that it is dangerous to put them
in a box which may never be found. Even if it is found,
the person who picks it up may not understand what he
is reading, and throw it away. Or he may be a criminal, 30
who will use the information in the wrong way.'

I paused and then went on, 'Could you not think of
another way in which to tell the world about yourself?
Could you not choose to allow us ...'

'Never, sir!' he said, interrupting me. 35

'But I and my companions are very willing to put your papers in a safe place. We will keep them as long as you like, and only publish them when you say. If, therefore, you would set us free ...'

'Set you free!' said the captain, rising in anger from his seat.

'Yes, Captain, set us free. That is what I wanted to ask you when I came in. We have been on board for seven months. Do you intend to keep us here always?'

'Professor Arronax, I will give you the same answer as I did seven months ago. Whoever enters the *Nautilus* may never leave it.'

'So you are making us your slaves.'

'Tell me what slaves are as comfortable as you. What slaves have work that is as interesting as yours?'

'But even slaves have the right to get back their freedom.'

'There is nothing to stop you. I did not make you promise to stay on board.'

He looked down at me from his great height, with his arms folded, and his mouth and eyes set in a severe expression. I do not know how I found the courage to say any more, but I did.

'I see. I will leave you now. But before I go, I would like to point out one thing to you. I am like you, because I am content to be busy with my studies. I would be happy to remain here for ever, in the hope that one day the world would know what I had discovered. But Ned Land is different. He will not remain here for ever. He will use force if necessary, in order to get free. He may even try ...'

'Let him try what he likes, but he will stay on the Nautilus, and so will you and your servant. That is all I have to say. Do not mention this subject ever again. I will not listen to you.'

Two hours later, the *Nautilus* changed course, and we set out across the Atlantic at a depth of 6,000 feet.

CAPTAIN NEMO'S REVENGE

Another secret

During the next two weeks we crossed the Atlantic. At first we were very sad, thinking that our last hope of safety had gone. We were also very much afraid that Captain Nemo would try to reach the North Pole, and so risk our lives again. After his strange behaviour of the last few weeks, we did not know what to expect.

Since I had made it clear that we wanted to leave the ship, and would try to escape, we expected that the captain would order some of his men to watch us carefully. But this did not happen. We were left to ourselves. The journey across the Atlantic followed a regular pattern. Things began to return to normal.

The nearer we approached to the coast of Europe, the more hopeful we became that we would soon have another chance. When we were off the coast of Ireland, the captain changed course to the south-east, and not to the north as we had feared. It seemed that we would soon see the shores of my own country, France.

But on 31st May the ship began to travel in circles. It was as though Captain Nemo was trying to find a particular spot. The sun was hidden by cloud that day, so our exact position could not be obtained. We remained in the same area, moving gently round and round.

The next day was clear. At midday the captain took the reading and announced with satisfaction, 'We are here.' Orders were given to descend, and we all left the platform while the tanks were filled with water, ready for the descent in the usual way.

As I moved to the staircase, I noticed another ship some miles away on the horizon. It seemed to be steaming towards us. I was a little surprised, because we were not on any of the regular shipping routes.

The *Nautilus* sank down and settled on the floor of the sea. The sliding doors opened, and we could see all round for a distance of some 900 feet. I noticed on one side of the ship what I thought was a large rock sticking up out of the sea bed. Then, after looking at it for a few moments, I recognized the form of a sailing vessel with no masts left. It had been on the sea bed for a long time, for it was covered with mud and seaweed. There was nothing else to see. Perhaps this was another treasure ship.

Just then Captain Nemo spoke. They were his first words to me since my conversation with him two weeks before.

'That ship was once called the *Marseillais*. It was built in 1762, and carried seventy-four guns. It fought in several sea battles, mostly in the West Indies and off the United States of America. After the French Revolution, it joined the navy of Admiral Van Staben. Exactly seventy-four years ago it was sunk. It was on its way to France, when it was caught by an English ship. Although the ship lost its three masts in the fight that followed, and one third of the crew were killed or wounded, the men fought on. Rather than give themselves up to the English, they preferred to die. The wreck that you are looking at is the tomb of 356 sailors who fought for freedom.'

'I know that story. The ship was given a new name. It was called the *Avenger*,' I cried.

'Yes, sir, the *Avenger*. A good name!' said Captain Nemo softly.

The way in which he said these words, and the way in which he looked at the wreck, made me wonder if this was another secret of this strange man. We knew that he was a brilliant scientist and engineer. We knew also that he loved freedom, and tried to help the victims of cruel governments. Was he also seeking revenge for something that had happened to him, or to his crew?

There was no time to think about this, for the *Nautilus* started to rise. Soon the rocking movement of the ship told me that we were on the surface. At that moment a loud, low noise was heard. Captain Nemo paid no attention, but I went up to the platform where I found Ned and Conseil already standing.

'What made that sound?' I asked.

'A ship's gun,' replied Ned.

The warship

The ship that I had already seen was very much closer to us now. Ned told me that it was a large warship, and that it was not flying any flag.

We first thought that this was a chance of escape. If the warship came within a few miles of us, we could jump into the sea and hope that it would pick us up. But as it came closer, it fired more shots.

'What!' I exclaimed. 'Are they shooting at us?'

'They recognize the narwhal, Professor,' said Ned. 'Captain Farragut must have reached port, and reported that the monster was a dangerous ship.'

'But if all the navies in the world are looking for this ship, why does that warship have no flag? And how did it know we were here? When I first saw it, it was sailing straight towards this spot. It must have expected Captain Nemo to come here. If so, that warship contains Captain Nemo's enemies. We shall be killed with him.'

'I will show them that there are good men on this ship,' said Ned. He took out his white handkerchief and was about to wave it, when he was thrown with great force onto the deck. Captain Nemo stood over him, his face black with rage.

'Fool!' shouted the captain. 'Do you wish me to tie you to the end of the *Nautilus's* sword before we sink that ship?'

He lifted Ned up and angrily shook him like a dog. Then he let go, and he looked up at the ship as it approached.

'Ah, ship of my enemies. You fly no flag but I know who you are. You know who I am and I will fly my flag. Look!'

He unwrapped the flag that we had flown at the South Pole. It blew in the wind. A shot struck the side of the ship and bounced off. The captain took no notice.

'Go down below at once, all of you!' he ordered.

'Are you going to attack that ship?' I asked.

'I will sink it,' was his reply.

'But that would not be right!' I protested.

'I will judge what is right, not you,' he said. 'You ought not to have seen this, but now you have. Go down at once. The attack has begun.'

'But what country does that ship belong to?'

'Don't you know? Then that will remain a secret. Go down I say!'

We had no choice. Fifteen of the crew stood beside the captain, all looking with the same hatred at the warship that came nearer and nearer. Another shot struck the ship but did no harm. As I went down, I heard the captain say, 'Shoot, enemies, shoot, but you will not harm me. I will strike you with my ship and not one of you will escape. But not here. I will not allow you to sink anywhere near the *Avenger.*'

How many other ships had he sunk, I wondered? And who were his enemies, and what had they done to him?

I went down to my room. The captain stayed on the platform. The speed was increased, and soon we were out of reach of the warship's guns. They began to chase us, but the *Nautilus* was easily able to keep away from them.

At about 4.00 p.m. I could not stay in my room any longer. It was not locked, so I went up again to the platform, and found Captain Nemo walking up and down. The ship was about six miles away and following him. I could not understand why he did not attack. Perhaps he still hesitated. Perhaps I could persuade him to leave the warship unharmed. I decided to try, but I had hardly spoken when Captain Nemo told me to be silent.

'I am the law and I am the judge. Because of those people I have lost all that I loved — my country, my wife, my children, my father, and my mother. I saw them all die! Those are the ones who killed them. I will make them pay for their crimes.'

I said nothing, but went at once to Ned and Conseil. We agreed that if we could, we ought to escape before the *Nautilus* sank the warship. We would not stand a very good chance of succeeding, but that no longer worried us so much. It was more important to avoid having any share in Captain Nemo's crimes, and to make at least some attempt to warn the men in the warship of their danger.

My task was to go to the platform, and watch for the best moment for us to throw ourselves into the sea.

Captain Nemo was there also, but he took no notice of me. Instead, he looked steadily at the warship. It was sailing at full speed. Clouds of smoke made the sky black. It was even possible to hear the noise of its engines.

All night the ships remained two miles apart. It was clear the *Nautilus* would not attack until day. But when dawn came, the warship attacked first. It fired several shots, but none came near us.

At about 7.00 a.m., the *Nautilus* began to slow down. Some men came up and took down the rails from around the platform. At any moment, it seemed, the *Nautilus* would rush towards the warship. We must be ready to jump into the sea.

I went down to warn Ned and Conseil. I found them both ready and both calm. I was so nervous that I could hardly stand. There was no one about. We moved through the library, then into the dining-room, and then into the centre of the ship. We began to climb the stairs. Just then the hatch closed above us, and we heard water pouring into the tanks. We were too late!

The warship sinks

I had expected the *Nautilus* to hit the warship on the surface, but it was going to strike it below water. In a few moments we were under the the waves. We could not avoid taking part in this crime.

I went with Ned and Conseil to their cabin, and we waited together. We listened for any sound. The *Nautilus* increased its speed. Very soon it was moving faster than it had ever done before. The shock of the crash had to come any moment. We held our breath.

Crash! We were thrown to the floor. We could hear the sound of metal scraping against metal. The *Nautilus's* engines continued to work. The ship kept moving. It was going right through the hull of the warship. Then the noise stopped. The *Nautilus* had made a hole in the side of the warship, just as easily as a needle makes a hole in a piece of cloth.

We rushed into the sitting-room. Captain Nemo was there, standing in front of the window, the doors of which were now open. His face showed no feelings of happiness or sorrow. We looked out too, and saw the dark outline of the warship. We could see the huge hole in its side. Water was pouring in, and the warship was sinking quickly to the bottom.

The side of the warship passed in front of us, two lines of windows, then the decks, then the guns. Last of all the masts passed us. Crowds of sailors were struggling on the decks. and hanging onto the ropes and the masts. Most had had no time to escape, and were being drowned where they were working. Some were free and swimming up to the surface. But no one escaped.

Suddenly there was a loud explosion, and a great burst 10 of flame. The ship blew up into pieces, and the shock was felt in the *Nautilus*. The warship went down, and all the men with it. In a few moments everything disappeared into the darkness below us.

I turned to Captain Nemo. He was still looking at the 15 place where the warship had been. Then he turned to his room and went in. I watched him walk to his bed and kneel down beside it, looking up at a picture of a young woman and two little children. He held out his arms towards them, and then buried his head in his hands and 20 wept.

Time to escape

The *Nautilus* continued its voyage at a steady speed. We had no idea where we were going, or even in what direction we were sailing. For fifteen days we went 25 on and on. The ship remained on the surface only long enough to renew the supply of air. Each day we went up to see if there was any land, but we could see nothing. The sky during that time was hidden by cloud and fog.

Captain Nemo stayed away from us. We saw no member of the crew. Nobody recorded the position of the *Nautilus* on the map.

The weather grew colder. Ned and I stopped going up to the platform, because we felt there was no point in looking at mist and fog. For all we knew, the ship might be going round in circles. We had both given up hope.

But Conseil continued to go up and look, and one day he told us that land was in sight. The effect of this news on both of us was amazing. At once we began to make new plans for escape.

We decided that we would make our attempt that night, when we might expect everyone to be asleep. We would have to use the ship's boat, and we hoped that the *Nautilus* would not sail too far below the surface. But even if it was in deep water, it was a risk worth taking, for certain death faced us if we stayed on board. Ned still had the tools for unfastening the screws, and Conseil had kept some food and water for our use.

There was one other decision that we made. If we were stopped, we would fight.

The hours of waiting seemed like days. I forced myself to eat, and stayed in my room. My notes were ready, and I did not look at them again. My thoughts returned to Captain Nemo. Where would he end his life?

When it was time to go, I moved into the sitting-room. To my horror Captain Nemo was there. He was playing the organ very softly. His back was towards me, so he did not see me come in. I walked step by step across the floor to the other side. I was ready to run the moment he saw me. Suddenly he got up and shouted very loudly, 'Almighty God! Enough! Enough!'

I moved more quickly than I had ever moved in my life. I reached the door and opened it. As I did so, I looked back at him. He was standing with his arms stretched up into the air. He was facing towards me, but he was looking up and did not see me. 5

Into the whirlpool

I ran through the library and dining-room, and rushed up the ladder. I crawled through the opening, and found Ned and Conseil already inside the boat.

'Let's go!' I whispered. 10

'At once!' replied Ned.

He closed the hatch in the roof of the *Nautilus* and then the hatch on the bottom of the boat. We were out of the *Nautilus* and inside the boat. All we had to do was loosen the screws that fixed us to the ship. 15

Suddenly we heard voices. Ned put a knife in my hand. We stopped undoing the screws and we listened. One word was repeated again and again.

'The whirlpool! The whirlpool!'

Then I remembered. We were off the coast of Norway. 20 Rushing between two islands, the tide makes a whirlpool that drags ships round and round, down to the bottom of the sea and breaks them on the rocks. This was the end which Captain Nemo had chosen for his ship, his crew, himself, and us. 25

We sat in the boat, waiting for death. After a few moments, we could hear the ship scrape on the rocks. Then it went up again, and round and round.

'Perhaps we will be safe if we stay with the *Nautilus*. The ship seems too strong even for the whirlpool,' said Ned. 30

'But we are getting short of air,' said Conseil.

At that moment, the screws were pulled loose by the force of the water. We were separated from the ship, and shot up at great speed. We were alone in the boat, and being shaken up and down with great violence. 35

I rolled over and struck my head on a piece of iron. I knew nothing more.

When I recovered, I found Ned and Conseil already awake and bending over me. I was not in the boat, but in a fisherman's hut. We were safe and sound.

A complete description

Now we are waiting here for a ship to take us to France. Ships do not come here very often, so we may have to wait for quite a long time. But we are free.

I have been looking through the notes I made of our adventures. I can truly say that not one detail has been forgotten or left out. It is a complete description of our voyage under the sea. By the time we reached Norway, we had sailed 20,000 leagues, and it had taken us eight months.

I sometimes wonder if I shall be believed. I do not know, and it does not really matter. One day, no doubt, people will see these wonders for themselves, and my story will be proved correct.

More often, I wonder what has happened to Captain Nemo. I wonder if the *Nautilus* escaped the whirlpool as we did. I wonder if the captain is still alive, and if so, what he is doing. I wonder if he has attacked and sunk any more ships in revenge for the loss of his wife and children. I wonder if one day someone will find his book on the sea shore. Perhaps then we shall know who he is, and from what country he comes.

I hope he is alive, and that his ship is still exploring the depths of the oceans. I hope, too, that he does not seek revenge any more. I hope that he continues to help those who struggle for freedom.

I lived with him for eight months under the sea. I saw the wonders that he showed me. Now there are two scientists in the world who can really describe what lives in the depths of the seas: Captain Nemo and myself.

QUESTIONS AND ACTIVITIES

CHAPTER 1

Put the letters of these words in the right order.

Professor Arronax thought that if it was a (1) **estmorn**, and if it lived near the bottom of the (2) **enaco**, it would have to be large and strong to resist the water (3) **seprerus**. The Professor thought it was a huge (4) **rhalwan**. The largest one caught up to then had been (5) **nytewt** yards long and had had a six foot long bone (6) **drows**, as hard as steel. The Professor believed the (7) **scindacet** at sea had been caused by a creature as strong and as powerful as a (8) **phrasiw**.

CHAPTER 2

*Who said these things? Choose from: **the Professor**, **Ned Land**, **Captain Farragut**, and **Conseil**.*

1 'I must wait until daylight, so that I can decide what parts to strike.'
2 'Before I dived into the sea, I heard some sailors say that the rudder was broken.'
3 'We can swim for a few hours, if we take off our clothes.'
4 'When I fell off the ship, I was lucky because I landed on this floating island.'
5 'These men are like savages. I expect they will eat us.'
6 'Wait until the men harm you, before you judge them to be bad.'

CHAPTER 3

There are eight mistakes in this paragraph. Can you find them?

The *Nautilus* used steam for the power needed to push the ship through the water. Electricity pumped petrol and water into the tanks, lit the ship and was used to cook the food. In the library there were some instruments which helped the captain to guide the boat. He could control the speed, depth and direction of the ship by turning a wheel, or pressing a bell. Captain Nemo had built the *Nautilus* by ordering different parts from different factories. He had put them together in a desert. The ship had cost sixty million dollars to build. The books had cost eighty million dollars, and the art treasures 200 million dollars.

CHAPTER 4

Use these words to fill the gaps: ***flowed, helmets, opened, lamp, heavy, screwed, bed, windows, fastened, carried, water, cabin, bottle, collar.***

The suits were uncomfortable, and very (1) _____. The (2) _____ were put over our heads, and (3) _____ down into a metal (4) _____. Each one had three (5) _____, so we could see in front and to each side. As soon as it was in place, a (6) _____ was (7) _____ to our backs, and air (8) _____ in. A gun and a (9) _____ were put into our hands. We had to be (10) _____ to the (11) _____. The doors shut behind us, and the room filled with (12) _____ When it was full, another door (13) _____, and we walked freely onto the sea (14) _____.

CHAPTER 5

Put these sentences in the right order to say what happened in the story. The first one is done for you.

1 Ned, Conseil and the Professor went to the Island of Gilboa to look for things to eat.

2 When the natives took hold of the handrail, they gave a loud cry and jumped back, and so did Ned when he tried.

3 Conseil and the Professor ran to the boat, and Ned came running after them carrying the kangaroos they had killed.

4 They lit a fire and began to enjoy a delicious meal, but then they saw about twenty natives.

5 The next day about five or six hundred natives came near to the *Nautilus* in their canoes.

6 There was electricity in the handrail, which gave a severe shock to anyone who touched it.

7 In the afternoon of the following day the crew opened up the hatch, and some natives tried to come down the stairs.

CHAPTER 6

Put the words at the end of these sentences in the right order.

1 Conseil thought Captain Nemo hated men because some people — [at] [ideas] [his] [laughed] [brilliant] [had].

2 The Professor said that if the Captain hated people, he would — [rescued] [not] [from] [drowning] [have] [them].

3 He wondered if there were some people he hated so much, — [wanted] [he] [to] [them] [destroy] [that].

4 Later, when the *Nautilus* was near Ceylon, Captain Nemo — [the] [to] [pearl] [took] [them] [fisheries].

5 The Captain saved a fisherman from a shark, and — [of] [him] [pearls] [a] [gave] [bag].

6 The Professor then understood that Captain Nemo — [some] [for] [still] [people] [love] [had].

7 The Captain said he had been cruelly treated, and tried to help — [suffered] [same] [others] [who] [treatment] [the].

CHAPTER 7

Choose the right words to say what this part of the chapter is about.

The *Nautilus* sailed right up to a (1) **volcano**/**cave** that was under the sea, close to the (2) **island**/**mountain** of Santorini. The temperature in the ship became uncomfortably (3) **cold**/**hot**. When Professor Arronax looked through the window in the (4) **sitting**/**Captain's** room, he could see that the water was entirely (5) **white/black**. Bubbles of gas were passing up through the (6) **air/water**, which appeared to be boiling. As the *Nautilus* sailed (7) **quickly/slowly** on, the water turned red. The Professor thought the ship would (8) **sink/melt**, and Captain Nemo agreed that it would be (9) **clever/unwise** to go on. He gave the order for the ship to change (10) **course/speed**.

CHAPTER 8

Put the beginning of each sentence with the right ending.

1 A mile around the *Nautilus*, the waters	(a) were clearing away old barrels and cases.
2 Some of the ship's crew, in their diving suits,	(b) would never be put to any good use.
3 The men were loading the treasure into new boxes, and	(c) were lit up by the ship's electric light.
4 The wrecks were Spanish ships that had been	(d) were treated unjustly by their rulers.
5 The commander had ordered his men	(e) caught by the English fleet in 1702.
6 Professor Arronax said that the treasure	(f) to burn the ships and sink them.
7 The Captain said he was using it to help people who	(g) bringing it back to the *Nautilus*.

CHAPTER 9

Which of these sentences are true? What is wrong with the false ones?

1 The *Nautilus* was trapped in the ice.
2 The only chance of escape was through the ice above them.
3 In twelve hours they cut out ice thirty feet deep.
4 At that rate, it would take them four and a half days to get free.
5 The Captain used the weight of the *Nautilus* to break through the ice.
6 They cut holes in the ice to make it stronger.

7 The reserve tanks were filled with air.
8 They heard a cracking sound, and then the ship was free.

CHAPTER 10

Use these words to fill in the gaps: ***seemed, stabbed, blinded, wrapped, wiped, screamed, prevented, spat, managed, attacked.***

What a scene we saw when we got outside! The unlucky man was high above us, held up by several arms which were (1) _____ round him. He (2) _____ in pain and fear. We (3) _____ the octopus that was holding him. We (4) _____ at it with our knives. The rest of the crew fought the other monsters and (5) _____ them from reaching the wounded man. At one moment it (6) _____ that we would save him, for we (7) _____ to cut off seven of the monster's eight arms. We had almost cut off the eighth when the creature (8) _____ out a stream of black liquid. We were (9) _____ by it. When we had (10) _____ the liquid from our eyes, the octopus had gone, taking the unlucky sailor with it.

CHAPTER 11

Put these sentences in the right order to say what happened in the story. The first one is done for you.

1 Professor Arronax found Ned and Conseil already inside the boat.
2 The Professor struck his head on a piece of iron.
4 He knew nothing more until he found himself on dry land.
5 They sat waiting for death as the *Nautilus* moved round.
6 They were separated from the ship, and shot up at great speed.
7 They heard people shouting about a whirlpool.
8 Then he closed the hatch on the bottom of the boat.
9 Then the screws were pulled loose by the force of the water.
10 Ned closed the hatch in the roof of the *Nautilus.*